T0131460

ATLAS

By: Asia Ifield

authorHOUSE®

AuthorHouse™
1663 Liberty Drive
Bloomington, IN 47403
www.authorhouse.com
Phone: 1 (800) 839-8640

Published by AuthorHouse 07/16/2018

ISBN: 978-1-5462-5100-2 (sc)
ISBN: 978-1-5462-5099-9 (e)

Library of Congress Control Number: 2018908154

Print information available on the last page.

CONTENTS

CHAPTER 1
WELCOME TO ATLAS INSTITUTION

MY MOM USED TO tell me about this place when I was younger. She even said it saved her life. She had me at the young age of 16. My dad was only 17. I spent my first four years living with my grandmother while my mom and dad trained here. Then, by the time I turned five my parents brought their first home! My mother explained to me how happy they were to finally be financially stable. A year later, my mother became pregnant with my little sister, Yvette. Now I'm 18 years old, Angel Myers, and my mom and dad sent me here, *Atlas Institution*. The place my mother claims, will shape my future for the better.

It was cold, empty and silent outside. It felt like the wind kept slapping me in the face. Moving my arms felt like I had wings as I couldn't keep them still. I stumbled over the big dark orange rocks surrounding us. I could barley look up, but when I did it felt as if I was having a mirage. I noticed Welcome signs surrounding a huge building that resembled a space ship, but fancier. I imagined this place be big but not this big! Luckily, I'm here with some friends from my neighborhood so I didn't feel so alone in this journey. We walked to the door in single file line with no idea what we were getting ourselves into. How exciting right?!

The circler shaped glass doors opened and we entered the building. Lights started flickering around us. We waited, thinking the doors would automatically open but never did. "What do we do?" Marley asked anxiously. "There has to be a way we get in here, we just have to..." Mike stumbles upon a pass code. "Just have to look for it!" Mike said as he searches for a call button on the pass code. Mike presses the button, "How may I help you?" A lady asked. "Hello, we are new students here and we're trying to enter the building," Mike replied. "Swoosh," the door opened, "Welcome to *Atlas Institution.*"

When I walked in, it almost felt like déjà vu. I just knew that I was in the right place. Everything seemed more advanced and high tech than what I'm used to on Earth. The students here seemed well mannered and put together. I also noticed guys in white suits patrolling the building. My group and I were escorted to a white room with one large white sofa. "You may all have a seat," A lady said. As she shuts the door behind her, the lights suddenly turned off. The sound of Broadway music starts playing. A TV turns on and comes down from the ceiling. The TV screen had a galaxy background with the words, "You're future starts here" going across the screen. The door opens. A women wearing a white trench coat walks in the room and turns on the lights.

The TV goes back up to the ceiling. "I bet you all were expecting a video, correct?" the women in the white trench coat asked. "Well I think I can speak for all of us when I say, we have no idea what to expect," My neighbor, Thomas replied. "Well to start off, you are in another universe so you should expect only, the unexpected," She said. She walks towards the center of the sofa. The sofa splits in half, making an oval shape surrounding her. "My name is Maria, and I am the CEO here at *Atlas Institution*," Maria proudly stated.

As Maria walked back to the front of the room, the sofa combined to its original form. "As you all know, you're youth clock has officially stopped as of today," Maria said. "What do you mean our youth clock has stopped?" Valerie asked.

That moment I heard someone whisper behind me, "oh no."

"Oh sweetie they didn't tell you?" Maria asked. Valerie was getting nervous, I could tell. Everyone was staring at her because they all knew something she didn't.

"Tell me what?" Valerie asked.

Maria shakes her head in disappointment, "I can't believe some parents make me break the news to their kids, how selfish. You know what; I'm not going to break the news this time, Maria looks over at us. "You are!" Maria said as she points directly at me.

"Me?" I asked that only in hopes that she would change her mind.

"Yes you, what is your name?"

"Angel," I stuttered.

"Angel... nice name...Please inform your classmate on the frequency of time here at *Atlas Institution*," Maria said.

If looks could kill I'd be dead right now. I didn't want to break this news to Valerie and scare her to death. I cleared my throat, "Time is frozen here.... Therefore you will stay at your current age until you pass the course, or as others like to say, "Graduate" and are able to return back to planet earth."

"Please explain to her in full detail," Maria ordered.

I sighed, "Time may be frozen here but it still continues on earth. So of course, when you do return to Planet Earth you will be older. You're basically graduating here and heading off to your future life. When you arrive... your life is as if you never left but, your level of success on earth is determined by your performance here at this school."

The room went silent. Valerie looked as if she'd seen a ghost.

"Ha, you're joking right?" She asked. I nodded my head but couldn't look her in the face.

She continued in rage, "This is a joke right? Why didn't my family tell me this before they sent me here?"

"They only wanted the best for you," Maria said.

"The best for me...how would you know what's best for me?"

Valerie jumps out her seat and rushes out the door.

"Oh, she's just making this harder for herself," Maria said as she walks over to the door and shuts it. I watched as Maria typed in some code on her tablet.

Seconds later and the alarms are activated. I could see men in suits running down the halls. Valerie has been my friend since middle school; I knew I had to do something.

I stood up and ran towards the door, "I have to go help her."

I pulled the door but it wouldn't open. The crazy part is the door wasn't even locked. It was as if there was a magnetic force preventing me from opening the door.

"I'm sorry; did you say you have to help her? Why would she need help; we are the professionals Angel," Maria said.

"But Valerie is my friend; I have to see if she's okay."

I pulled the door even harder this time and it still wouldn't budge.

"You're only going to make it worse Angel; leave it to the professionals, they deal with this all the time," Maria stated.

I didn't like the feeling of being trapped. I'm the one who broke the news to her, so shouldn't I have been able to talk to her after the fact. Maria stood there and watched me struggle to open the doors.

I stared banging on the doors out of frustration.

"Here we go," Maria said as she pulls out her phone. She starts typing in numbers.

"Wait!" Thomas interrupted.

Thomas grabs my arm before I could bang on the door.

He whispers, "Angel, just keep it cool okay, Unless you want guys in the white suits to come in here and do who knows what."

"Oh, so I'm just supposed to sit here and wonder what's going to happen to Valerie?" I asked.

"Valerie will be fine, trust me," He replied.

"Do you really believe that?" I asked.

"Yes, trust me. It's only our first day here, everything will be just fine," He replied.

I took a couple steps back from the door. I looked over at Maria and she's smiling. Two women walk in wearing matching outfits. "Now that that's over…This is Christy and Kelly; they are your personal tour guide for the day," Maria said. Christy and Kelly were two very energetic woman in their late 20's. "Hello Everyone, are we ready to check out your new school?!" Christy yelled. Everyone just sat there. "Oh uh, I need to wake you guys up! I said, are you ready to check out your new school?!" Christy repeated. "Yea!" Thomas yelled. Kelly ran over to Thomas and gave him a high five, "Yea! That's what I'm talking about! Who else is ready?!" She yelled. Everyone began to cheer as if nothing happened.

The first place they took us to was the cafeteria. The cafeteria looked more like a hangout spot. There are TV's in the center hanging from the ceiling, a white table fit for ten with turquoise chairs below it, and large booths with iPods on each to place your food order. "I know you all must be hungry, so grab something to eat then we will continue the tour," Christy announced.

I walked over to the vending machines and noticed nothing but healthy and organic food options. I was in the mood for junk food after a crazy morning. I took a seat at a booth and glanced through the menu. Thomas and his friend Ryan took the seats next to me. "This... can't be real," I said as I'm scrolling through the menu. "I'm really about to cry right now," I continued.

"I told you not to worry about..."

I interrupted Thomas, "There are only healthy and organic options on this menu."

Thomas reaches for the ipod, "No way!"

Thomas set the ipod down on the table.

"That's it, I'm done... my life is over," I said in desperation.

"Is it that serious?" Thomas questioned.

His friend Ryan takes a look through the menu, "Nooooooo!" He whimpered.

"You feel it too?" I asked.

"No more chilly cheese fries," Ryan whimpered.

"No more sprinkled donuts," I cried.

I put my head down on the table and pretended to cry, or maybe I was really crying.

Thomas gets up from the table. I lift my head up notice Iris taking Thomas's seat. "What's wrong with you guys?" she asked.

"Take a look," I said as I handed her the Ipod.

"What, this is... this is the best thing I've seen all day," Iris said with a big smile on her face.

"But no more chilly cheese fries!" Ryan said.

"Good…. the healthier rout is better for your body," Iris replied.

Thomas walked back over with a tray of food.

"Here, Ryan I got you a bison burger and Angel I got you a grilled veggie wrap."

I guess I had no choice but to try it being that this is what I was going to have to get used to.

"Let's wrap it up everyone!" Kelly yelled. "Now I know you all must be used to your typical classroom learning environment, but here is more hands on training," Christy explained as we walk through the halls. Christy opens a classroom door and said, "Hope no one is afraid of animals." We walked in to an indoor zoo… or more like jungle! "This is not real right now," I said in shock. A baby Monkey crawls over to Kelly, she picks him up. The classroom instructors walk over. "Everyone this is Albert, the classroom instructor and certified veterinarian," Kelly announced.

"Hello everyone, here in my classroom we are learning animal behaviors, researching medical conditions, and the simple act of nurturing our animals," Albert explains. I looked up to exotic birds flying over my head. The ceiling was extended.

We walked over to a small room in the back of this enormous classroom. "This room here is our animal care medical office," Albert said. Each student was wearing purple scrubs. We stood around a student giving a shot to a baby tiger. The baby tiger was very active and wanted to play. The other student in assistance attempts to hold the tiger down, so the tiger could take their shot. Gasp! The student accidental sticks the shot in the baby tiger a little off balance, causing the tiger to bleed. "Oh my gosh," Jocelyn said. The tiger starts to whimper. "What are we going to do? We can't just watch this happen, he needs help" Jocelyn continued. The students start laughing at Jocelyn. "No, no don't worry. In this medical office we do not treat real animals, only fake replicas. I know and realize that my students are not ready to perform real medical assistance," Albert replied. Jocelyn sighed in relieve.

A few of us students waited in the hallway for everyone to exit the classroom. "Feel free to take a look through the windows at the other classrooms besides you because we don't want to interrupt," Christy said. I took a peek through the classroom with a "Knock First" label on the door. The students wore lab coats and goggles. I noticed food containers all across the room. "Iris come look at this." Iris walks over and peeks through the window, "Oh this is my class!"

"Ahh, consumer testing… good choice," Christy said. Iris has been an advocate for healthy food choices since I met her. She watched her father suffer with different medical conditions she claimed was caused by all the fast food her father ate. Her face was glued to the window as she watched the students test the food products.

We walked further down the hall. So far I've seen a wide range of classes such as; landscaping, cosmetology, graphic editors, electricians, engineer's and etc.

"Here at *Atlas Institution*, we like to have all career options available for students," Christy explained. "Now, for those who rather take the traditional rout… there is the option for you as well. As you can see here, these classrooms are for mathematics, English, history, science, and foreign languages," Kelly said. "Yes… that is true but these aren't just your regular core classes. Mathematics students study for accounting, stock, and money management. English majors typically become journalist. History usually leads to politicians. Science has a wide range of chemical science, human development, environmental science, and the list continues. And last but not lease, foreign language students are more likely to become translators. Each one of these classroom teaches you the basics, but it is your choice to further your studies in the listed courses" Christy explained.

I watched as Thomas was fascinated with the Mathematics class. "Wouldn't everyone need to take these core classes?" Thomas asked. "Yes.. good question. Each student will take only the basics.. But as I explained, those who want to advance will do only if they choose to. Also, a class that is well recommending to students is business management," Christy said.

"Now it's time to show you guys the art department," Kelly said. The art department had its own entrance leading to a hall of beautiful paintings and sculptures. We entered a room with mirrors surrounding us. "This space is for dancers," Christy said. "Can I just stay right here? I think I found my home," Marley said. "This isn't even the best part,"

Christy replied as she opens the door on the other side of the room. We walked up a flight of stairs; the lights were dim. We entered through large red curtains; that's when I realized we were on stage. "This is our center stage, were every performer makes their debut," Christy said.

After leaving the art department, we were heading to sports and other athletics. "This is where you will find your gym if anyone likes to work out," Kelly said. Kelly opens the door, "Here is…" Ryan runs inside the indoor field before Kelly could even finish her sentence. He had a wondrous look as he ran to the field. "Yeah baby, my kingdom!" he yelled as he beats his chest. We all began to laugh while watching him dance with triumph. "I see we have our next football player," Christy said.

"Now, we are going to have to be very quiet when entering this hallway. This area is generated for our future doctors, and the other side is for our future lawyers," Kelly said. "We have to stay extremely quiet because these students obviously have more studying to do than the average student here. They go through an intense amount of training for this program that takes longer than most programs," Christy whispered as we entered the hallway. "Future Doctor here," Jocelyn commented. Jocelyn was my sister's best friend. She graduated earlier than others because of her high test scores. "Future Lawyer here," Mike proudly stated. Mike was the guy you grew up with that claimed to know everything. In reality, he pretty much did because he read up on his facts. I was happy to see him pursuing Law education so he could finally argue with other people instead of us.

"Alright Students, that was the end of our tour and I must say it was a pleasure meeting you all. Does anyone have any questions before we part ways?" Christy asked.

"What's on the second and third floor?" Mike asked.

"That's basically the next level of training. It has the same layout as the first floor but it is more advance. That's why you all on the first floor are mainly all new to the school," Christy said.

"What happens if you don't pass the first floor?" Iris asked.

"Simple, you stay here until you do," Christy replied.

"And what if you just keep failing and never pass?" Iris asked.

"Well, those students have two options. They could ether work for *Atlas Institution* or go back to earth homeless. Being that you never passed, your future is nonexistent as if you were never here. But, none of you have to worry about that, you all seem like bright students," Christy replied.

Kelly hands each of us a piece of paper. "Kelly is passing out your schedule for tomorrow's first day and if you look at the top of the page you will find your dorm room number. Right now, it is dinner time so go eat and enjoy, and you have any other questions fill free to go to counselor's office right down this hall," Christy said. "I just want to say you all made a great decision by choosing this school and we are excited to watch each and every one of you grow into successful young adults," Kelly said. Christy and Kelly waved good bye, "Thank you everyone!"

It felt good to sit down after that long tour. Thomas once again ordered food for me because I couldn't decide. "Still no sign of Valerie, I'm getting worried," I said. "Don't be, I told you, she's fine don't worry," Thomas replied.

"I sure do hope so."

"So did you see any classes your interested in?"

"Soo many, I don't know which to choose at this point,"

"I say, go where the money is at,"

"You would say that," I replied as the food arrived to our table.

He ordered me a chicken creaser salad.

"But hey, you're not the only one who can't decide. I heard the twins can't decide ether," Thomas said.

I looked over at the Nikko and Nikki. They were the neighborhood twins that really didn't talk much, but stayed to themselves. Everyone always thought they were weird but I think they are just misunderstood for being different.

I looked up at the television screen, "Oh my gosh that's my parents!" I said. "Oh and there's my mom!" Thomas said. The TV was airing old graduations from former students. My mother graduated and became a nurse and my father became an electrician. Now the only thing I had to think about was what was I going to be?

After dinner I searched to find my door room. I peeked through the other rooms and the rooms were pretty spacious for three roommates. "What's your room number?" I asked Iris. "I33" she replied.

"Hey me too!"

"Marley what's yours?" I asked.

"Umm, Room 135" She replied.

"Isnt that right there," Iris pointed.

"Ahh, my room!" Marley replied as she opened the doors.

Iris and I followed in excitement.

"I am in love with these rooms!" I said as I gazed over the futuristic layout.

"I know right, I wonder who I'm rooming with," Marley said.

Nikki and Nikko walk in at that moment.

"Oh, it's the twins. I'll see you guys, I'm going to go find our room Angel," Iris said.

"Hey, how did you like the tour?" I asked the twins.

"Umm, it was okay, I just didn't see anything I was really interested in," Nikko replied.

"What about you Nikki?"

"Same."

"Really, nothing?"

"Nope," They both said.

"Okay, well I'm sure you two are going to find something you're that fits your interest," I said.

"Doubt it," Nikki replied.

I started to feel awkward at this point.

"Okay, well I hope you all have a great night, bye Marley."

"Bye, goodnight," Marley replied.

I finally made it to my room. The lights were off and everyone was already sleeping. I turned on the lights quickly to find my bed. I wanted to get a glimpse of who my other roommates were. "Valerie?" I questioned. I gasp, "Valerie, oh my gosh!" I sat down on her bed but she was sleeping. I had to find out what happened to her today. I tried waking her up, "Valerie, its Angel." She tossed and turned. "Huh, I didn't do anything and I'm ready to leave," Valerie was talking in her sleep.

"You're ready to leave?" I questioned.

"I don't need to take any pills I need to call my parents," Valerie continued to talk in her sleep.

"Valerie, what are you talking about?"

"I don't want it. She said"

"Valerie?"

I tried waking her up but she didn't budge. It was weird because she is usually a light sleeper. I gave up after a while and got ready for bed. I was happy and relieved to know Valerie was okay. Besides the whole incident with her, I could say my first day here was successful.

CHAPTER 2
FIELD DAY

As soon as I woke up, I wanted to check on Valerie. I walked over to her bed and she wasn't there. The bathroom door opening nearly petrified me. Valerie stands there with a towel around her & her slip on shoes. "Good Morning," Valerie said with great enthusiasm.

"Valerie, what happened yesterday? I asked with no hesitation.

"What do you mean?"

"Yesterday, after you stormed out the room?"

"Oh yea, nothing… they ended up giving me food because I missed lunch, then they showed me my room and fell asleep,"

I was utterly confused at how she was reacting as if nothing happened.

"Everything okay?" I asked.

"Yea girl, I'm ready to choose my classes! Why aren't you getting dressed?"

"Umm, okay. I guess I'll get dressed right now." I took a couple steps backwards.

Valerie turns on some music. I went in the bathroom to take a shower. I slightly opened the door to see what Valerie was doing. She was dancing and putting on makeup. I turned the shower on. I sat on the toilet to let the water run, then found myself thinking of how weird Valerie was acting. I slightly cracked the door open to see what she was doing; she was still dancing and putting on makeup as if nothing ever happened.

It didn't take me long to get dressed. I put on some burgundy flare pants and basic pink top. I met up with Thomas for breakfast. I couldn't wait to talk to him about Valerie. We eat eggs and toast for breakfast while watching the news on earth. How we get signal to be able to watch this… I'm not sure but watching the news sure did make me glad I got a way for a while.

"Oh yea, and about Valerie, I spoke to her this morning and she acted like nothing even happened," I told him.

"Maybe nothing did happen," he replied.

"No, my gut is telling me something different."

"I don't know why you're stressing it. You wanted to make sure she's okay and she is so….what's the issue now?"

"The issue is, I don't believe her story and I think something else happened that she doesn't want to tell me."

"But she tells you everything, why would she start keeping secrets from you now?"

"I don't know, that's what I'm trying to figure out."

"Anyway, did you decide on what classes you're going to take?"

"Not even, I wish I could have a trial run for the few classes I'm debating on taking."

Ryan rushes in our direction, "Hey all new students are meeting in the auditorium," He said.

We entered the auditorium; it was already packed with students. I took the empty seat next to Valerie.

A man walks on stage with a microphone in hand, "Good Morning students!"

"Good Morning….." We all replied.

"My name is Mr. Jamison, I am the principal here at *Atlas Institution,* and I just want to congratulate you all on making the best decision of your lives!"

The crowd cheers. "Today is a big step for you all, as you are deciding your classes. Or more like, deciding your careers. I do have a surprise for those who haven't made up their mind yet. This year we are doing things a little bit different by introducing, field day! Field day is when you are able to choice a multiple amount of classes and test each one to gather a feel of each class. For those who've already made a decision on the classes you want to take, great… but for those who haven't, this is your chance to make your mind up. Now I'm sure you all have met the lovely ladies, Christy and Kelly," Mr. Jamison points as Christy and Kelly make their way to the stage. "Christy and Kelly are going to hand out a list of each class and an envelope. For those that are choosing field day, please check that box along with the classes you're interested in taking." Christy and Kelly grab the list and envelopes then make their way back down stage. "Remember students, you're future starts now; choose wisely," Mr. Jamison said.

I looked at the list of over 30 classes; it was starting to give me anxiety. Valerie started checking in her boxes immediately as the list was given to her. The only box I've checked so far was field day. "Everyone you have two minutes to finish up," Christy announced. I took a deep breath and just winged it. "Times up everyone please seal your envelopes and pass them down the row," Christy said. "Oh shoot, what if I made a mistake?" I thought. I quickly scanned through my list. I couldn't think straight. If my choices were based off what I loved doing but would that even benefit me in the end. I thought of what Thomas said, "Go where the money is". I erased most of the choices on my list and quickly checked in some different ones. I sealed my envelope and passed it down the row. "Thank you everyone, you may head to your core classes. After lunch we will have schedules for everyone," Christy announced.

Pretty much everyone I knew was in my first core class, mathematics. "My heart is still pounding you guys," I said. "Why, are you nervous?" Marley asked. "Nervous, anxious, happy, mad…I really don't even know how to feel," I replied.

"What classes did you decide?" Thomas asked.

"I'm not going to say, but I am participating in field day… I know that," I replied.

"Is anyone else?" I asked.

NO one replied. "So everyone in here knows exactly what they want to do in life?" I asked.

"Pretty much," Mike replied.

They all began to laugh.

"Not us," Nikki said.

Everyone silenced as Mr. Jamison walks in.

We all wondered why the principal was in our class and if he was looking for someone.

"Hello again students," he said and put his belongs down on the teacher's desk.

"I know you all are probably thinking, what's going on right now?" he asked.

"Well, surprise... I'm going to be your mathematics teacher," Mr. Jamison announced.

I wondered if I was the only one nervous about the principal being our teacher.

"Don't worry students you don't have to be afraid, I'm only here to help you succeed," he stated.

"So what made you decide to be a teacher and principal?" Marley asked.

"Well, I started off as a teacher here and then made my way up to principal but I just couldn't leave teaching," He replied.

"Any other questions before we begin?" he asked.

"How long have you been teaching here?" Marley asked.

"Pretty much all my life. I studied here when I was about your age, then went back home and became an official teacher. I got married, had kids...but after a year of being married my wife divorced me and took the kids. So, I came back here and I've been here ever since."

"You don't miss your family?" Iris asked.

"Of course I miss my family but there was no hope of making admen's with my ex wife so I rather be here, teaching and staying fairly young," Mr. Jamison replied.

"How old would you be, if you don't mind me asking?" Iris asked.

"Around 57, 58 I believe."

Right now, he could pass for the age 30. I couldn't believe how someone could be away from their family for that long.

"Did you cheat?" Marley asked.

The class was shocked Marley had the balls to ask that question.

"Sorry, I just want to know," Marley said.

Mr. Jamison chuckled, "Oh no, it's okay. Yes, I did cheat."

"And she didn't forgive you?" Mike asked.

"She did, yes...then I made the mistake of cheating again," Mr. Jamison replied.

"Shiiiiiiiiiiiiit, can't nobody take me away from my kids. Not even my ex wife," Mike said under his breath.

"Okay, does anyone have any classroom related questions?" Mr. Jamison asked.

"Nothing? Okay, let's begin," Mr. Jamison said as he hands out the curriculum.

After long classes of mainly talking and explaining, it was finally time for lunch.

This time I sat with the girls: Iris, Valerie, Marley, and Jocelyn.

I ordered another Cesar salad; I wasn't sure what everyone else was getting.

"What are you doing Marley?" I asked as she kept looking around the cafeteria.

"I'm trying to scope out some cute guys up in this place," She replied.

"Ha, good luck with that," I said.

"Really, because I see some cuties over there."

"Oooo who, I want to see," Iris said.

"Sitting right there by the vending machines," Marley replied.

"Okay she's right, they are cute," Iris replied.

I looked over to see, "Oh okay, where have they been this whole time?" I asked.

"I don't know… but I want to find out," Marley said.

"Why don't you go over there?" I asked.

"Me, why me?"

"Because you spotted them," I replied.

"Why not Jocelyn, she can go over there," Marley said.

"Oh no way.. I'm too shy for that," Jocelyn replied.

"Valerie?" Marley asked.

"Not interested," Valerie replied.

"Iris?" Marley asked.

The cafeteria worker brings over our food.

"Nope, food over boys is what I always say," Iris replied.

"Really?" Marley replied.

"Yes, really," Iris replied as she stuffs her mouth with roast chicken and sweet potatoes.

"Fine, I'll just go over there myself," Marley said.

Marley takes a dollar from her purse and puts it in her pocket.

We watched her as she makes her way to the guys table. She walks straight pass them and goes to the vending machine.

"Oh she's not going to do it," I said.

"Yea, I doubt it," Iris replied.

"I don't know...she sounded pretty confident about talking to them," Jocelyn replied.

Marley grabs her veggie snack out the vending machine.

"Let's see if she has the guts," Iris said.

Marley turns to the guys table and starts chatting with them.

"Oh well look at her," I said.

"Hmm, I guess she does have the guts," Valerie replied.

Marley was leaning on the table smiling from ear to ear.

"Oh she's coming back," Iris said.

Marley makes her way back to the table.

Out of nowhere the guys in white suits approach Marley.

We all Gasp. "Is she getting in trouble?" I asked.

"No way!" Iris replied.

"Uh, well it doesn't look like a pleasant conversation," Jocelyn said.

Marley walks away with the guys in suits.

"Oh yea...she's in trouble," Iris replied.

"But where are they taking her?" I asked.

"Who knows," Iris replied.

I looked over at Valerie to see her reaction. You could tell she didn't want to get involved with the conversation but I had to know.

"I bet Valerie knows," I said.

"Knows what?" She replied.

"Where are they taking her?"

"I don't know...probably the principal's office. That's where you go when you get in trouble at school right?" Valerie sarcastically stated.

"Yes, but this isn't just your average school if you haven't noticed," I replied.

"Right, well.. maybe they are just going to have a talk with her," Valerie said.

"So, no junk food, and no boys, I'm curious to find out what next," I said.

"Yea, I don't think you should be curious about that one," Jocelyn replied.

The bell rings, I felt a sudden knot in my stomach.
"You alright?" Iris asked.
"Yea, I'll be fine. It's not like my whole life is on the line right now,"
"Don't worry, all you have to do is work hard and be decisive,"
"Be decisive? I'm a Libra," I replied.
"Well, you need to make up your mind and fast. I want to see you in a couple years on earth doing big things,"
"I know, I know."
"Good luck and… work hard!" Iris said as we all went our separate ways.

Christy and Kelly were sitting at a table outside the cafeteria with our schedules listed. I grabbed mine and read at the top of the page in big font letters, "Field day".

I entered a hallway with teachers standing outside each door. The first class on my list was Information technology, or as other like to abbreviate it, "I.T". This class was on my list of classes that would make me a lot of money but I had no idea what it was even about. I stood in line to enter the classroom. The teacher was introducing himself to each student.

I didn't take me but a couple seconds to reach the front of the line. "Hello, I'm Mr. Franklin," He shakes my hand then hands me an envelope. "Once you enter the class room you may open the envelope and begin," He said. I walked in the classroom and it was empty. There was only one desk in the middle of the room. I quickly turned around and the door disappeared. The whole room was empty with just one desk surrounded by white walls. It felt as if I was the last person on this planet.

I almost forgot about the envelope Mr. Franklin gave me. I flipped the envelope over and it read, "Take a seat". I took a seat then opened the envelope. I took out the piece of paper and read: In this class room you will be un-coding and designing. Your first assignment is to make you're self comfortable and design your own layout for this classroom. Once finished, unlock the code given to you at the end and enter the classroom.

Different classroom layouts appeared in front of my face on a square shaped screen. I decided on the layout with blue walls and diamond shaped sculptures on the ceiling with different equations listed. I changed our desk from regular classroom desk to a space age office desk. I then changed the layout of the class room from a square flat layout, to oval shaped layout. The student's desk was spread out through the classroom with their own personal space. The teacher's desk was clear and in the center of the classroom. My last finishing touch was a globe of the earth circling around the classroom. I looked over my design the pressed finished. I was then given 5 minutes to unlock a code to enter the classroom. The code was a bunch of numbers that looked like equations. I followed the code pattern and attempted to unlock it. I heard beeping sounds, "That is incorrect". I have three minutes left, the code seemed like jumbled up numbers at this point. I couldn't see straight under this much pressure. I copied the code once more. I read the instructions again before attempting to unlock it. I only have ten seconds left. My fingers never typed so fast. I hit enter, Beeeeep, "You are correct," I unlocked the code.

The white walls dissolve around me into a regular classroom setting. My classmates were appearing one by one around me. My Franklin stood at the front of the class and waited for each student to unlock the code and enter the classroom. After everyone arrived he gave us a minute to get settled while he did some work on his laptop. "Welcome again students," Mr. Franklin said. I have reviewed each and every one of your class layouts, here are the top five," He continued. Mr. Franklin takes out his tablet and swipes right.

The first layout had bright orange walls and pop art everywhere. "It's colorful, vibrant and creative. Well done," Mr. Franklin said. He swiped right again and the room changed from a colorful bright orange to an under the sea classroom. It was very creative but I could see it being a distraction as fish swam in front of my face. "This layout is most advanced layout I've ever seen in my years of teaching here. Way to think outside the box," Mr. Franklin said then swiped right. The next class room nearly scared me to death as I put my feet out to thin air. We were up in the beautiful sky with the world at our feet. "I like this idea but I really just wanted to see how the rest of you students would react to this. Overall, great job," Mr. Franklin said. I looked up and an earth globe speed past me; it was my classroom layout. Mr. Franklin looked at me and smiled, "This classroom is innovated and inspiring." He swiped right once more, the classroom went back to its original layout. "But I thought it was between five layouts?" A student asked. "That is correct, this last layout is for the students who said the classroom should stay a regular classroom," Mr. Franklin replied. "But this is I.T, the most advance class here, we need a layout that will explore our minds and challenge us for the future," The student replied. "So which layout did you have in mind sir?" Mr. Franklin asked. "I really liked the last layout with the globe circling around us and equations over our head," The student said. I was completely shocked he spoke about my layout. "Anyone have a problem with that being our classroom layout?" Mr. Franklin asked. The students didn't disagree. Mr. Franklin swiped away on his tablet and the classroom was back to my layout design.

- "Of course you all may know, what we performed today were virtual layouts. This is similar to Web Developer. In the world of "I.T" there are varies jobs such as Web Developer, I.T consultant, Cloud architect, Computer forensic investigator, Health I.T specialist, Mobile application developer, software engineer, and the list continues. Whatever it is you are doing it is important to gain that visual imagery. To act as if your walls at home or in your office come to life as you are designing. Must successful students here have a passion for computer technology and are able to sit at their computer desk for a long period of time. Other students just come here to make a lot of money, then flunk because they simply get weary from looking at a computer screen all day. Please, save yourself the trouble and decide wisely, because this is your future," Mr. Franklin said.

The rest of the classroom period we sat at our computer desk typing away. I caught myself ether looking at the time or looking at the world globe circling around me. The field day bell alarms, it was time for the next class. The sound of the bell never sounded better. "Angel, before you leave," Mr. Franklin stopped me. "This layout you created was a fantastic idea."

"Thank you, I took deep thought into it," I replied.

"I see, you have a great visual imagination that I believe will get bored in this classroom," He said.

I sighed because he was right. He walked me out the classroom. "I noticed you often staring at the globe or the time. Now I could be wrong, and this could be you're future career but I need you to make that decision for yourself. You are very talented Angel, " Mr. Franklin said. "Thank you," I looked back at the classroom I designed and smiled, "I'll think about it," I replied.

I walked into my next class, "podiatrist". I didn't know what that meant; I just knew it was on the list of highest ranking jobs. I walked into the classroom and smelled a strange aroma I couldn't seem to classify. I watched as students grabbed their gloves and head the back, so I followed. Once I saw the first old man with his shoes off and the room smelling the way it did I was turned off. Turned out "Podiatrist" is a foot doctor. You couldn't pay me enough to touch peoples feet all day. I walked right back out of that classroom.

The next class on my list was to be a certified dentist. Once again, I was in line to grab gloves before entering the class room. I walked in the back and the students were holding false rotting teeth. I sat at an empty desk and picked up the false teeth in front of me. The false teeth were a splitting image of real teeth. They even carried the smell of real rotten teeth. I opened the jaw and started looking through the teeth. The strong smell made me realize my dentist wore mask. "Now, we are going to take each tooth and label them accordingly," The dental instructor said. "Do we have any mask?" I asked. "Yes, here you go," The instructor said as she handed me the mask. "Couldn't take the smell?" She asked. "Not at all," I replied. "Well, these teeth belong to an elder woman who smoked cigarettes nonstop and didn't take care of her teeth as you can see," She continued. I dropped the teeth out my hand, "So these are real?" I gasp. "Yes, we want to give you the real situations you will run across as a dentist," The instructor replied. I thought I was about to throw up. I don't think I could work in a field with hygienic problems; my stomach couldn't take it.

My next class was the television industry. At first I couldn't enter the class room because there was a big red sign saying, "Filming in progress". As soon as the red lights turned off I walked inside. The class room was more like a TV set. I sat in the audience wondering where the rest of the students were. "Alright everybody, are you ready for the greatest show in television!" The announcer guy said full of energy. The crowd cheers. "Alright, welcome to the stage, you're host... Emily Anderson!" The crowd is going crazy as Emily walks on stage. She does a cute little dance and waves at the camera. "Alright, today on this show we are sitting down and..." Emily stopped after she missed up her lines. The announcer guy comes back out, "Alright, Emily is going to give it another try so can we have the same energy as the first time!" Emily walks back off stage. The announcer guy continued, "Alright everybody, are you ready for the greatest show in television!" The crowd cheers. "Welcome to the stage, you're lovely host... Emily Anderson!"

Emily walks on stage and stumbles on the rug. The audience was waiting for her to begin hosting but she never did. "Thank you so much Emily," The announcer guy said. "Alright, whose next?"

A woman in the audience stood up, "I'm next."

To my surprise the audience was all students who wanted to be in the television industry. There are almost 300 people in this one class.

The announcer guy explains, "For those of you who just entered this wonderful classroom/ tv set, my name is Jorge Jimmy, and I am your teacher! Can we all clap for Emily for going on stage and being so brave?" He asked. The crowd cheered for Emily.

"Now in this class as you can see you have a lot of competition; But when this is something you love doing the competition shouldn't matter. I know this is probably the biggest class you guys have ever been in but you can't let that effect you in this business. In the world of television you are amongst millions of people all around the world, basically. I've been teaching here for many years and I've seen the class go from 300 students to only 100 students. I've seen students give up before they even begin because the competition isn't what they are used to. Now if you really love hosting and the film industry you must know this is only for people with strong backbones. You won't always get the opportunity you want and most of the times it's all a waiting game for your big shot," Jorge explained.

Pop music began to play and Jorge left the front stage. The TV set went from a live talk show setting to a broadcast channel. The audience was silent. Jorge came out in a suit and tie with a head piece in his ear. "Alright, thank you all for being quiet on the set. In 5,4,3,2......"

"Good Morning *Atlas Institution*, I'm Georgina, and today we are discussing the issues which lies here on *Atlas Institution*." The promoter shuts off, Jorge signals Georgina to keep going. Georgina continued, "The first issue lies with the cafeteria food, I mean who eats healthy all the time…" The crowd laughs. "And cut!" Jorge said. "Sometimes students you will be placed in predicaments that you will have to improv the scene or in this case, headline. Great job Georgina," Jorge said.

I was entertained every minute of this class, but I was getting irritable from waiting for my turn. The bell rings and I still haven't gone on stage. I didn't want to leave the classroom. I waited for everyone to leave to stand in the center of the set. As soon as Jorge exist the class room I made my way to the stage. "Good Morning *Atlas Institution*, my name is Angel and I will be you're host this afternoon, today we are talking about the issues here at *Atlas Institution*," I took a seat on the coach. "Let's talk about the guys in the white suits; I mean who are they, and what do they do?" I said. I heard the door opening. "And that's all for today's segment of Angel News, I'll see you next time," I said then ran towards the door. I left of out the side door before Jorge entered through the front door.

I sat in the room of my final class for field day. The class room didn't have desks, only round tables. The instructor walks in and a large screen starts scrolling down. "So you want to be a Psychiatrist" Read on the screen. I enjoyed helping people and didn't mind talking to them about their problems. This job is listed as one of the highest ranking jobs in the US. The instructor puts on his reading glasses. "Good Evening Students, my name is Rachel Jean and I am your instructor. You can call me Rachel, you can call me Jean, you even called me RJ; I don't really give a shit. In this class we are studying human behaviors, diagnostics, and treatments," Rachel said. I looked around to notice about 50 students, 2 of them being Nikki and Nikko.

"Psychiatrists are also known as medical doctors. We often treat patients with great pain or discomfort. I know most of you here are planning to go into the therapy field. That field is used to treat the mental ill as well as your average person going through problems. We in fact, are often people's last resort when we should instead be there first. People tend to come to us when they are on the last straw or after anxiety attacks. We then help our patients overcome such illnesses and traumas.

For the rest of the class I sat there and listened to Rachel speak. It was boring, but the information given was starting to get interesting. When the classes ended I was in much relieve to finally be over with field day. Now the hard part was deciding which class I was going to take. I walked into the cafeteria and sat at the table with the rest of the girls.

"How was everyone's first day?" I asked.

"Kill me," Jocelyn said as she laid her head on my shoulder.

Everyone else sat there in exhaustion.

"You know what, why don't we all have some fun tonight?" I suggested.

"Fun? Yea, good luck with that," Marley replied.

"No really, let's get together with the guys and do something tonight."

"Like what?" Valerie replied.

I whispered, "Well, I have chocolate, gram crackers and marshmallows in my dorm room."

"So you're trying to make S'mores, where though?" Jocelyn asked.

"Outside…" I replied.

"Are you talking about sneaking out?" Jocelyn questioned.

"Oh no, oh no no no," Valerie replied.

"Yea, I'm not down with that ether," Marley said.

"Why not, no one is going to find out," I replied.

"This placed is filled with cameras. How are they not going to find out?" Marley replied.

"We can go in the back, and run to a pit somewhere," I replied.

"And how are we going to get back in?" Jocelyn asked.

"I saw a back door through the arts department, we can leave it open," I replied.

"There's no way that's going to work, I'm out," Marley said.

"Me too," Valerie seconded. Both her and Marley get up and leave the table.

"Iris and Jocelyn, you two down?" I asked.

"Hey, I'm with it. I need a break after today," Iris replied.

"I guess I'm in too, I just have never done anything bad in my life soo," Jocelyn said then laughs nervously.

"Don't worry Jocelyn, you'll be fine," I replied.

I flagged Thomas down to join us at the table.

"Wassup?" Thomas asked.

"How about and your roommates join us tonight for a bonfire?" I asked.

"A bonfire, what about…"

I interrupted Thomas, "I have thought of everything possible, don't worry."

Thomas shrugged his shoulders, "Well okay then, 'I'll let them know," Thomas replied.

I go into my room and grab all of my treats for tonight's bonfire. Jocelyn, Iris and I put on our all black clothes and got ready. Valerie headed for bed.

"You sure you don't want to join us Val?" I asked.

"Oh I'm positive," she replied then put her head back on her pillow.

We waited for the lights to shut off in all the hallways. We quickly opened the door and were startled by Nikki and Nikko.

"What are you guys doing?" Nikki asked.

"We're having a bonfire tonight, you two want to join?"

"Why not, we're already dressed in all black," Nikko replied.

"Finally something fun around here," Nikki whispered.

We tip toed through the halls to the art department. We stood there by the door. "Come on guys, where are you?" I said nervously.

"We're here, we made it," Thomas replied.

"And we have lighter fluid. We took it from the chemical science class," Mike said.

"Alright let's go," I said then opened the doors.

We used a metal door stopper to hold the door open. We all took off running as soon as our foot touched the ground. We tried finding a secure spot. We stopped after 2 minutes of running and not being able to feel our fingers from the cold. The guys set up the bonfire while the girls snuggled together for warmth. As soon as the fire lit, we started making s'mores. "I can't believe I'm doing this right now," Jocelyn said.

"Aww, Jocelyn isn't used to breaking the rules huh?" Mike commented.

"No, I don't go around stealing lighter fluid like you do," Jocelyn replied. We all started laughing.

"So how is everyone doing?" I asked. You could hear crickets because no one wanted to say anything.

"Is everyone shaking up from their first day?" I asked.

"Well when you think about our future success rate based on these classes, it is kind of nerve wrecking," Thomas said.

"Yea, tell me about it. At lease you guys know what you want to do. I have to make a choice by tomorrow," I replied.

"Well what do you want to do?" Mike asked.

"I love entertaining people, I love helping people, and I also love making a lot of money" I replied.

"What happened to Valerie and Marley; they didn't want to come?" Ryan asked.

"No, they've been shaken up every since the guys in the white suits said who knows what to them," I replied.

"You're still on that," Thomas said.

"Yes, I am. Until I find out what happened I'm not going to let it go," I replied.

"I don't think you're wrong, something is fishy around here," Nikki replied.

Everyone gasp. "Well well, look who decides to finally speak," Mike replied.

"We do speak for your information… you are just never around," Nikki replied.

"Well can I be around, because I would love to get to know you," Mike said.

"Uh, no," Nikki replied.

"ha ha, Looks like Mike can't always have what he wants," Iris said.

"Anyone miss their families already? I really miss my mom," Jocelyn asked.

"Man, I would kill for my mommas cooking right now," Ryan said.

"Hey me and you both, you're mom makes the best steak and shrimp pasta," Mike said.

"What about you two, you miss your family back home?" I asked Nikki and Nikko.

"You mean our grandmother? Yea..."

"What about the rest of your family?" I asked.

"We only have our grandmother because our mother and father both passed away," Nikki said.

"Wow, I'm sorry," I replied.

"It's okay, our mother and father went to school here so it's almost as if they are here with us," Nikki said.

After a long night of laughing and telling stories, we started heading back inside. We ran back to the door and it was barley open. We walked in one by one then suddenly the lights turned on. We ran to hide. I noticed everyone but Mike and Ryan, they were stuck outside. The guys in suits ran outside and grabbed them. I felt so bad for them because this was my idea. We waited for the guys in suits to leave and turn off the lights.

"Thomas, this is all..." I began to say.

"Don't, this isn't your fault we all wanted to do this," he replied.

"Please tell me in the morning what happened?"

"Nothing is going to happen, Good night Angel."

"Good Night."

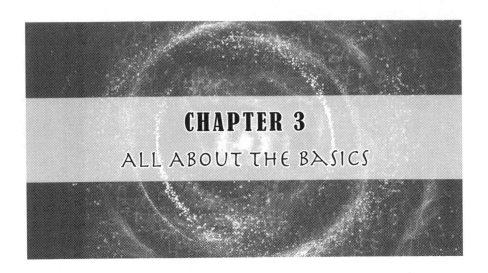

CHAPTER 3
ALL ABOUT THE BASICS

I MET UP WITH Thomas for Breakfast. "So tell me everything, what happened?" I asked.

"There's nothing to tell, nothing happened," Thomas replied.

"They weren't acting strange or anything?"

"No, by the time I was in the room they were already there sleeping. When I woke up this morning they didn't say anything about it."

"Hmmm."

"No, it's not hmm, nothing. I'm telling you, you need to let it go."

"Yea, maybe... but not until I figure out what pill this is they are taking."

Thomas flags Ryan over to the table.

"Wassup man, ready for another day of training?"

Ryan shakes Thomas hand; "Yea man!" then walks away.

"You see, normal," Thomas said.

"That proves nothing," I replied.

"So which class did you decide to take?" Thomas asked.

"I still don't know..uhh," I replied.

"What, you had a whole night to think about it," Thomas replied.

"I know but it's not that simple. Not everyone can be like you and know exactly what they want."

"You can actually, if you just make a decision."

"This isn't just a decision Thomas. This determines if I'm poor class, middle class, or wealthy, and I think I'll choice to be wealthy," I replied.

"You can be wealthy in any career choice if manage it properly,"

"Did you learn that in business management?"

"I did, are you even taking that class at lease?"

"I am."

"Are you ready for Mr. Jamison's class?"

"Yea... I am actually, what about you?"

"I guess... the guy seems like he has issues though,"

Thomas and I laugh as we headed to class.

Mr. Jamison hands out a piece of paper to each student.

"Using math in the real world is more than just calculating. It takes money management and smart spending to actually maintain your funds. This assignment given to you is instructed as followed: Students will be given 50,000 to start their business/ investment. Students are held accountable for each dollar spent. Students will be evaluated at the end of the assignment based on their chosen business/ investment," Mr. Jamison read to the class. "Fifty thousand dollars," I said in shock. "Yes, I will be giving each student fake money that very much resembles real money. Remember students, 50,000 is a lot of money but it can go to waste if you don't spend wisely and correctly." Mr. Jamison said.

Everyone immediately began working on the assignment. "Oh and one more thing, the student with the highest ranking predicted investment will receive 25,000 to start business in real life. So, by the time you get back to planet earth, 25,000 will already be in your savings account. This assignment has changed lives for many students so please take it seriously," Mr. Jamison announced to the class. "Can you believe this?" I whispered to Thomas. "This is a dream come true. I told you this school had a lot to offer, you just had to give it a chance," Thomas replied.

After my core classes was over, it was time for me to head to my career choice based class. I stood in the hallway while many thoughts ran through my head. "Do I do what I love that I might not be successful in, or do I get a job that is garneted to make me a lot of money?" I only had 2 minutes to decide because the late bell would ring by then. I finally made a decision and headed to class. The late bell rang as soon as I took my seat.

"Today class we are learning all about the basics," Mrs. Rachel said. Mrs. Rachel makes her way to her desk and grabs a handful of papers. "I am going to be handing out the basic procedures you will need to follow in this class. You will also be receiving a psychology book. Each student is required to type every definition listed in this book before you leave my class," Mrs. Rachel said. She opens a box containing about fifty, five hundred page books inside. She passes the books out to each student. "Now students, after reading the basic procedures you may start by readying Chapter 1 in your psychology book.

After what felt like thirty minutes reading, my eyes could barley stay open. I have a short attention span and I just couldn't seem to focus on this book. I wondered what TV production class was up to right know, although that isn't what I wanted to think about. I wanted to focus on psychology to become a therapist. I wanted to be able to help people with their issues and also make a lot of money.

I sat in the cafeteria by myself during dinner. I had too much on my mind and I wasn't really in the mood to talk to anyone. I put my binder out on the table and started flipping through my notes. Only my first day of my official classes and I already felt overwhelmed. My mother never said this journey was going to be easy, but she also didn't mention it was going to be this hard. "Keep working, it'll all pay off" Is what I constantly had to remind myself. I would be devastated if I returned back to planet earth working a minimum wage job and not be able to afford to live a fulfilling life.

The next couple of days here were pretty much the same routine. I was learning the basics in psychology, working on my project for mathematics, and my other core classes were basically memory knowledge. I was passing all my classes so I would say I was doing pretty well. Psychology was my lowest grade and that was a B minus. I barely had time to speak to my friends. Everyone kept their focus on school. At night, before heading to bed I always tried to catch up with the girls to see how things were going. Jocelyn was learning the basics for the medical field, Iris was in the stage on identify different chemicals, Valerie barley speaks to me and nor does Marley. Every since their talk with the guys in the white suits they've been acting different towards me. The other girls didn't believe me; they claimed they were just too busy.

I sat on my bed and started typing up the definitions for psychology class. Jocelyn had her earphones in and was getting ready for bed. Valerie walks in the room and sets her books down. "Hey Val, wassup?" I asked.

"Nothing much, just going to get some studying done," She replied.

"How is class going?"

"Fine,"

"Just fine?"

Valerie shrugs her shoulders, "Yup, just fine."

"Is there something you're not telling me? Why are you being short with me?"

Valerie looks at me and smiles, "No, I am just eager to learn and advance in my career that's all."

I sarcastically reply, "Okay, well you have a great night friend," and went to bed.

Valerie and I have been friends for way too long for her to be treating me this way. I knew I had to get to the bottom of this.

I turned my lamp on and continued typing away on my computer. After finishing with my definitions, I started studying investments for Mr. Jamison's class. With my fifty thousand dollars I was going to start my own fashion line. I had the idea for a fashion line because everyone loves clothes and I had a great sense of style. I started doodling on a piece of paper for my designs. After a couple of designs, I needed to come up with a brand name. I thought of names all night until I fell asleep.

"Alright class, today we are having a pop quiz" Mrs. Rachel said.

I didn't like surprises, especially not from my psychology teacher. I've been studying though, so I was somewhat confident. "We are going to watch a video of a child with mental health issues. After the video it is your job to diagnose the student. I don't expect all of you to get it correct because this is going a head of what we have learned, but I want you all to be prepared for the 2nd floor. 2nd floor psychology is all about diagnostics and it will not be nearly as easy as this class," Mrs. Rachel announced. My classmate nudged me and asked, "Who said this was easy?"

The video started playing. The girl in the video acted like a regular girl. She was in walking the hallways of a school. When her classmates approached her, she smiled. I didn't see anything wrong with her. We watched her in class, learning and copying notes like the rest of the students. She raised her hands, than asked her teacher if she could use the restroom. She walked in the bathroom stall and completely lost it. She started silently screaming and crying. She took a pen and started writing all over the bathroom stalls. She then pulled out her pocket knife and cut herself. I was completely shocked. After a couple minutes of her cleaning up the blood she went back to her class. She took her seat and smiled at her friends as if nothing happened. After the class period was over she met up with a group of friends by her locker. She was laughing, smiling and looked as if she was fine.

The video ended. I stared at the piece of paper in front of me. I felt like that video didn't give me enough information, and I needed to see more. "Alright students, you have five minutes," Mrs. Rachel said. I sat there thinking. Nothing seemed wrong with her until she went to the restroom. Or maybe, nothing "seemed" wrong with her but she let all her emotions out when she went to the restroom? I had so many thoughts running through my head. I even tried to put myself in her shoes. "You have two more minutes," Mrs. Rachel said.

I started writing down everything that I could come up with. I rushed as Mrs. Rachel was collecting the papers. "Now students, we are going to watch the second proportion of this video," Mrs. Rachel said. The girl was sitting in a room, across from a therapist. "So tell me what's going on?" The therapist asked.

The girl sat there without a reply.

The therapist then said, "Whenever you are ready to talk."

"I can't answer your question," the girl replied.

"Why is that?" the therapist replied.

"Because I don't know what's going on, I don't know what's wrong with me."

"Is there something that triggered this feeling?"

The girl paused and thought about the question. Tears started rolling down the girls eyes.

"This is just me, I guess. I don't know what's wrong with me," She said.

"Are you willing to open up more so that we can get to the bottom of this feeling?" The therapist asked.

"Yes," the girl replied.

"First things first before we start I need to ask you, are you feeling the need of hurting yourself or anyone else?" The therapist asked.

Mrs. Rachel turned the TV off.

Gasp! "Why'd you turn it off?" my classmate asked.

"Because, we got all the information we need for our quiz," Mrs. Rachel asked.

"And what's that?" my classmate asked.

"Hmmp class, sometimes you are going to have patients that have no idea what is wrong with them and it is our job to help them find the source of their pain. These are obvious signs of depression but we don't know what type, or if she is dealing with any other issues. The point of this assignment was to show you all that we are not going to have the answers right away based of the client's actions and it is very important not to judge but to speak and get to the bottom of the issue," Mrs. Rachel said. "What happens if she isn't ready to open up?" I asked.

"Well, typically they prescribe her with medicine that will help her get through the days until she is ready to have that conversation with you," Mrs. Rachel said.

"Medicine? There is medicine to cure with mental illness?" I asked.

"That is correct, medicine that helps you function rather than drowning in negative thoughts and depression," Mrs. Rachel replied.

The bell rings. "Oh, one more thing students," Mrs. Rachel said as we gathered our belongings. She grabs the quiz papers and rips them in half and, "You will all receive an A today for this assignment." The class cheered. "Go get some food and have a great night students," Mrs. Rachel said.

Tonight for Dinner I ate fish, rice and corn. I needed a full meal after a long day. Jocelyn sat at the table with me with her Chicken pesto pasta. We sat there for a while without speaking. "A lot on your mind," Jocelyn asked.

"Yea, you too?" I asked.

"Just class, and getting ready for the 2nd floor" She replied.

"It's going by so fast," I replied.

We burst into laughter.

"I mean, of course it would feel this way," Jocelyn said.

"What's on your mind?" Jocelyn asked.

"Psychology class today has me thinking about life," I replied.

"How so?"

"Well to start off, someone can look completely fine on the outside but be completely damage on the inside."

"Yea.. in the medical field we sadly deal with patients that had mental illness and their parents would have no recognition of it at all."

"So sad…. Then as therapist we are suppose to prescribe our patients with medicine to help them recover. So they are basically swallowing their pain in a pill…" I began to say. I stopped speaking after noticing Valerie and Marley sit at two separate tables by themselves. "What if….?"

"What if Valerie and Marley are on some type of pill that is making them react the way they do. Valerie even said something about a pill in her sleep that same night," I questioned.

"Then there's also…" I started looking for Mike and Ryan. When I spotted Ryan, he was eating cabbage… just plain cabbage. "Oh heck no, something is wrong here," I said. I jumped out my seat to go look for Mike. I walked the halls, looking for Mike but I ran into Iris. "Where you headed?" Iris asked.

"I'm looking for Mike, have you seen him?"

"No, sorry I haven't"

"Do you want to help me find him?"

"Sure… why not."

We walked in the school library. Mike was in the back, studying for pre law. I whispered to Iris, "I dare you to go over to Mike and tell him you want him."

"No way I'm not doing that.. and get his hopes up, hmmp," Iris replied.

"I'll give you ten dollars," I suggested.

"You're really going to pay me ten dollars to go up to Mike and tell him I want him?" She asked.

"Yup," I replied.

"Okay.." Iris starts walking towards Mike then suddenly pauses and turns around.

Iris said, "So you just want me to say, Mike I want you or what?" She asked.

"Yea, yea, yea… just like that is fine," I tried to rush her before Mike noticed us.

I was hiding behind a bookshelf near the table Mike was sitting at.

Iris walks over to Mike and takes a seat beside him. "Hey Mike," Iris said.

"Hi Iris," he replied.

Iris looked back at me and smiled after Mike continued to type of his laptop.

"Mike…. I want you," Iris said.

Mike stops typing on his laptop and slowly looks over at Iris. "Thank you for the compliment," Mike said.

Iris was lost for words, "okay," she said.

Iris gets up from his table and Mike didn't even look back after she left.

Iris stands on the corner of the book shelf. She whispered, "I guess he's too busy."

"Too busy? When has Mike ever been too busy to try to talk to you?" I asked.

"Iris Gomez? The guys in white suits sneaked up behind Iris. I quickly hid so they weren't able to see me but I was still able to see and hear them.

"Yes, that's me.." Iris replied.

"Unfortunately your recent actions here have not met our standards here at *Atlas Institution*," A gentleman in his white suit said.

"What… what do you mean?" Iris asked.

"We need you to come with us," They replied.

Without giving Iris a chance to respond, they are taking her away. I followed behind them.

They ended up taken Iris to a room with hospital beds spread out throughout the room. My heart is pounding as I'm watching through the window. They lay Iris down on the hospital bed. I then heard the sound of high heels coming in my direction. I ran in the nearest closet. The tapping from women's high heel grew louder; I heard Maria's voice. "What did she do?" Maria asked.

"She broke rule 227 in our regulations ma'am," A man replied.

"Ahh, poor girl…. It happens," Maria replied.

I waited in the closet for a while, waiting for the perfect moment to escape. A grabbed the door knob. I started to gently open the door until I heard Maria voice once more. I quickly shut the door.

"Our only choice was to treat her with the pill; it was for her own good. She would thank me in the long run if she only remembers," Maria said as she begins laughing.

I opened the door. I peeked through the room and Iris wasn't there. I quickly left the hallway and went looking for Iris.

As I'm walking through the halls, a bunch of students are walking towards me. "What's going on?" I asked one of my classmates.

"The CEO is calling for a night meeting," She replied.

I followed the students down the hall to an exit outside. I took a seat outside and waited for the meeting to begin. Maria walked over to the podium and waited for the students to silence. It was cold and windy and outside. Luckily there were patio heaters outside.

"Hello Students!" Maria yelled.

"Hello Mrs. Maria," the students replied. I looked around at the students and most of them looked warn out.

"I know it's going to take a minute for everyone to adjust to this school but I believe in each and every one of you…. But, I must address some issues that have been surfacing. Each student must obey the rules and guidelines we have here at this school. Those who break rules will receive disciplinary actions against them and no one wants that. Know that everything we do here is only for you to be stronger and ready for the future on planet Earth. Know that we are only here to help. Does everyone understand?" Maria asked.

The students replied in unison, "Yes Mrs. Maria!"

"Now it's time for the good news," Maria said. Confetti cannons blew in the air. Balloons appeared above our heads. Maria presses a red button on the podium, releasing the balloons. "Congratulations students for making it to the 2nd floor of training! You have survived the 1st floor and now it is time to take it to the second level!" Maria announced. "Here at this school we like to congratulate our students along the way of achievement. You're future… is bright," Maria announced then walked off the podium. I noticed Christy and Kelly handing out books to each student. After given the book the student was dismissed to leave and head to bed. "Here is your book Angel; be sure to read every page because we wouldn't want you to get in trouble," Christy said. I grabbed my nook then headed back to my room. When I walked in it wasn't a surprise to find Iris already in her bed, sleeping.

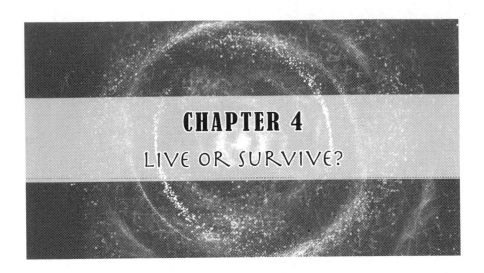

CHAPTER 4
LIVE OR SURVIVE?

I WOKE UP TO my roommates packing their bags. "Its move out day," Jocelyn said.

"Don't worry, classes are cancelled today for us to move to the 2nd floor of training," She continued. "Is Breakfast the same time?" I asked because that's all I cared about at the moment. "Yes, breakfast is the same time... I was about to leave in a minute," Jocelyn replied. "Okay well that's where you'll find me," I replied. I freshened up a bit, and then headed to the cafeteria.

I really wanted to speak to Thomas about how I felt about this place, but I was tired of trying to convince him about something he didn't believe.

"Ready for the 2nd floor?" Thomas snuck up on me and asked.

"I have no choice but to be ready right?" I replied.

"Yea.. Accounting is kicking my butt right now," Thomas said.

"Well at lease you love it."

"Love it, who told you that lie?"

"That's what you wanted to do since the day I met you."

"No, my parents had me make a choice between jobs and this was the only one I could tolerate. This is what is going to provide for my future kids."

"Aww, you want kids?"

"In the future... I would love them... (whispers) but let's not talk about that before we get in trouble."

"Why would we get in trouble?"

"You didn't read the rule book?"

"Not yet..."

"Rule 277 states no PDA, talk about future kids, or sexual acts towards anyone here."

"Explains it..."

"Explains what?"

"Nothing..." I continued eating my breakfast.

"See you on the 2nd floor," Thomas said.

I walked back to an empty room. My roommates have already cleared their belongings. The sad part was I came here with most of my friends but now I never felt more alone. I packed my bags. I sat there on my bed thinking. I grabbed my suitcase and left the room. I ran to the elevator, it was packed with students. The second floor was slightly different from the 1st. Each student was given an envelope with their name on it. I opened my envelope to find my new schedule and dorm room number.

I walked in my new dorm room and stood at the door amazed. My room had stars as the wallpaper and all white beds. It looked as if the beds were in the middle of space. I found my bed and set up my belongings. I heard knocking on the door, it was Nikki and Nikko. "Looks like we are roommates," Nikki said. "Oh... well I guess we are," I replied in surprise.

A digitalize note appears in the middle of the room on thin air.

The note read, "Press here to open".

I pressed on the note and it unfolds.

"Welcome to 2nd floor training" the note read at the top of the page.

Nikko reads the rest of the note: "Now it's time to step it up a notch. As you may have known you are placed with roommates who share the same career profession as you. The reason behind this is only because birds of a feather flock together. It is important to surround yourself with people who share the same mindset as you. The time is now; because you aren't going to be given this chance again in your life time... spend it wisely."

After reading the note it vanishes.

"What a way to welcome us huh?" I stated.

I turned around and Nikki and Nikko were already gone. I walked in the hallway and there were arrows pointing in one direction. Above the arrows read, "2nd floor tour this way". Once again there was Christy and Kelly, standing there with their fake smiles and cute outfits. "We meet again students for another tour," Christy said. We follow Christy's lead down the hall.

"Now, this tour isn't going to be as long as the first one because the 2nd floor is the same layout as the first," Christy explained. "The catch is that each class is more advanced," Kelly said. "You all remember the first class of our tour on the first floor correct? Well, here is the same class but on the 2nd floor," Christy said. She opened the classroom door. The instructor passed Demanet training bite suits and helmets to each student before entering the room. I heard a large growl through the doors.

I walked into a more advance indoor jungle filled with wild animals. I left the group to look around because it was so interesting. Suddenly a tiger starts charging at me. I started running. I kept running thinking I would find a door to exit but the jungle was never ending. I hid behind a tree and started running in the opposite direction. From a distance I could see the students from my tour group. I couldn't scream through my mask, so that wasn't an option. The tiger appeared in front of me. I had nowhere to run. The tiger takes full charge at me then runs straight through me. The instructor and his students walk towards me. "Oh dear, did you really think the students here would be ready for real wild animals?" He asked. I stood there still in shock. He started laughing, "That's only on the third floor."

We took a mini tour of the 2nd floor. We stopped at the athletic center. Students were training in martial arts and self defense. Other students were working out and lifting weights. "This room is going to become your best friend when you have 3 exams due, 2 projects and you just need to relieve some stress," Christy proclaimed.

We walked down the hallway. "Another room you guys will find helpful is the yoga room. We are about to enter the room but I must warn you, you have to be completely quiet. Any sound made and you will be escorted out the room," Kelly said.

We entered a hot and sweaty yoga room. Each student had their eyes closed and legs crossed. The bell rings and the students get into a different position. This position was on their back with their legs in the air. The bell rings once more and the students inhale and exhale while putting their legs on the floor. We exit the room. "Now students you are given more freedom on the 2nd floor because we expect more from you all. So you are more than welcome to tour the rest of the floor but we are going to get some lunch," Christy said.

I decided to skip lunch today and tour the school. I walked into the counselor's office. The office was empty with a sign, "gone for lunch" on the front counter. I headed to the back of the room to the head counselor's office. I heard the sound of a television. I tapped my fingers nervously. I wanted to check it out but I was afraid. I opened the door. I walked in and followed the sound of the television. The head counselor's office contained files on each student. The TV was playing a video of a woman at her job. I took a second glance at the TV and the woman looked awfully familiar. There was a folder on her desk with the name, Stacie Hopkins labeled on it. I glanced through the folder. The folder stated her career choice and grades. I closed the folder and the TV suddenly turned off. I opened the folder again and the TV turned back on. I read through the folder: Stacie Hopkins, future telemarketer. I flipped through the pages in her folder; I then saw a current picture of Stacie. Stacie Hopkins was the girl in my mathematics class. That's when I realized I was looking at her future on the television screen.

I quickly closed her folder then looked for mine. I opened my folder. There I was, a therapist treating one of my clients. After my client left I sat there with a blank facial expression. I grabbed the remote and pressed fast forward. I watched a glimpse of my future life. I didn't look very happy, I looked unfulfilled actually. I pressed play. I watched myself cry at my therapist desk while looking out the window. "Maybe I made I mistake... Do I really want to become a therapist?" I asked myself.

I closed my folder and looked for my friends folders because I didn't have much time. I found Mike's folder next. I opened it and he was a happy lawyer. He had a wonderful family, and beautiful home. I closed his file and opened the next file closest to me. It was Ryan's file. Ryan made the NFL draft. I fast forward and his team made it all the way to the super bowl. I couldn't be more proud of him. I skimmed through the game; I couldn't help myself. It was the last quarter of the game and his team was winning. I watched the next play as Ryan ran with the ball. Ryan team mate falls, leaving him wide open. Ryan gets knocked out by a defensive player. I fast forward and Ryan was still on the ground. I didn't want to see him hurt so I continued to fast forward. I watched him in the hospital bed after the doctors explain to him how he is going to need crutches. A year later and Ryan never returned to the team. Ryan never fully recovered so the team let him go. Ryan then worked at a fast food restaurant; he was in his late 40's by this time.

I suddenly heard the bell ring, lunch was over. I ran out the room. By the time I reached the front, the counselors were already entering the room. I hid behind a desk and waiting for each of them to go to their office. The receptionist took her seat. I was stuck in this one spot. The receptionist then noticed she forget to take the "Gone for lunch" sign down. The receptionist got out her seat and I ran to the front door. When opened the door and she heard me and turned around. I quickly closed the door. "Hi, sorry I ran in here," I said. She starts laughing, "Yea, you were pretty fast I didn't even notice you. How can I help you?" She asked. "I wanted to know if I could get a copy of my schedule?" I asked. "Yes ma'am you can, Angel right?" She asked.

"Yea, that's me…how'd you know?"

"Oh we know the names of all the students here, that's our job," She replied.

She printed my schedule and handed me the copy.

"Thank you," I said.

"If you have any other questions don't be afraid to stop by," She replied.

I headed to the gym because I needed to let off some steam. I turned my music on and hopped on the tread mill. I didn't view my classmates the same nor this school after what I saw. I tried tuning into my music but it didn't work. I walked into the virtual running room with treadmills to be completely alone. The virtual running room is let you decide which setting you would like to run in. I decided to run outside. I turned the temperature to cool air. I put the sun down and raised the moon. I turned my music on blast and started running.

I stopped at the virtual athletic park. I put some boxing gloves on and started punching the nevatear heavy bag. Images of my future kept appearing in my head and I couldn't shake it. I just started punching harder and harder. After my workout I left the virtual workout room. I headed to my room and was stopped by Jocelyn on the way there.

"It's only been one day and I feel like I haven't seen you in forever," Jocelyn said.

"Yea, I know... sucks we can't be roommates anymore," I replied.

"How do you like your new roommates?"

"My new roommates and the twins, Nikki and Nikko."

"No way, I didn't know they were in your major."

"Yea, so where are you headed?"

"Back to my room, think I'm going to head to bed early tonight."

"You're not going to dinner?"

"No, I think I'm going to skip dinner tonight...I don't have the appetite."

"You don't have an appetite, are you sick?"

I laughed, "No, I'm not sick... I just need to sleep things off at the moment."

"This doesn't sound like you... have you been with the guys in the white suits?"

"No, and don't say that too loud."

"Ouuu I'm scared."

"Jocelyn, since when have you become so tough?"

"I don't know...this school just made me realize only the strong survive. So I had to gain tough skin or be left behind."

"You know what, you're right..."

"Does that mean you're joining me for dinner?"

"Yea, it does...let me take a shower first then I'll meet you there."

After a quick shower I headed to the cafeteria for dinner. I tried to clear my mind at the moment and just enjoy my dinner. I watched Ryan and Thomas walk in the cafeteria. I hoped Thomas wouldn't notice me and continue walking. The cafeteria lady accidentally bumps into Ryan causing him to fall to the ground. I watched him fall and flash backs appeared in my head of him getting knocked out at the super bowl game. Ryan luckily got right back up, but I lost my appetite.

"I'm going to head to bed Joce."

"Aww soo soon?"

"Yea, at least I showed up right?"

"Yea... I guess." Jocelyn chuckled. "Sleep well tonight and try to meditate if you have too... release any negative energy," Jocelyn said.

I left the cafeteria before Thomas could say anything to me.

I walked in the room and I was the only one here. Maybe now I could take Jocelyn's advice on meditating. I put my yoga mat on the floor. I sat there in silence for a couple minutes. I inhaled and exhaled several times. The image of my future popped in my head. I shook my head, trying to think of anything else possible. The image was still there. I inhaled and exhaled once more. I then painted a different picture in my head; this image contained the future I imagined. I was happy and peaceful but I still didn't know exactly what I wanted to do with my life. If I controlled my future although, I would have a plan on how to figure it out. Something suddenly clicked in my head as those thoughts ran through my mind. If I controlled my future I would not just survive in this world, but I would live.

I woke up the next morning with positive energy and a refreshed mind. My first class of the day, was 2nd floor mathematics. Mostly everyone from the 1st floor made it to the 2nd floor. We sat there waiting for the teacher. Mr. Jamison walks inside. We were all wondering what he was doing here. "Hello, students...did you miss me?" Mr. Jamison asked. "I am pleased to announce that I will be your 2nd floor mathematics teacher and we will be continuing the assignment as if you never left," He announced.

"How are you able to teach the 2nd floor?" A student asked. "Well students, I have decided to go back home after the 3rd floor training. It is almost as if, I am graduating with you guys," He replied. "But wouldn't you be too old to return back to earth?" A student asked. The class took a long gasp, waiting for Mr. Jamison to reply. "Yes, I will be Farley old... maybe even in my 70's, but I decided nothing is worth my happiness. For me to be happy, I need to see my children," He explained. The class began to clap. "Alright, alright...back to work students," Mr. Jamison said.

Just like my mathematics class, my psychology class was as if I never left. The set up was the exact same. I turned around and noticed Nikki and Nikko sitting the back of the room. A woman walks in the room. She was tall and slim with long blonde hair. "Good Evening students, I am your new teacher Mrs. Jenkins," She announced. "Your last teacher had a lot of good things to say about you, so my expectations for you all are fairly high. Today we are going to learn about the different medicine for different diagnostic," Mrs. Jenkins said. She put a picture of different pills on the screen and the benefits description bellow each.

We copied the list on a piece of paper. "I have a question," I raised my hand and said.

"Yes?" Mrs. Jenkins asked.

"I'm not sure if this is a stupid question or not but are there such things as bad pills?"

"First and foremost, there is no such thing as a stupid question. Just elaborate on your question for me so that I am able to answer it correctly."

"I know there are pills to help people but are there pills out there that harm people as well? Like for an example, are there pills that can put people in a depressive state instead of taking them out of it?" I asked.

"Unfortunately not all pills are used for good. That's why it is very important to be couscous over everything you take or give. Some pills can cause you to even lose your state of mind and in those cases it is very difficult to return to your original state of being," Mrs. Jenkins explained.

After class I walked over to the counselor's office. This counselor's office had someone on duty at this time. "Can I help you with something?" The receptionist asked. "Oh no I was just taking a tour of the 2nd floor. I wanted to stop by the counselor's office then I realized I was never given a tour inside. Is it possible for me to look around?"

"No unfortunately not, students are not allowed behind those doors," The receptionists replied. "Okay, thank you…" I replied then headed to the door. "One more question. Is the counselor's office available for students at all times?" I asked. "No, we are not available during or after dinner time hours," She replied.

"Okay, thanks again" I replied.

I waited in the restroom minutes later before dinner time. After the bell rang, I walked back over to the counselor's office. I tried opening the door but it was locked. I felt defeated. I walked down the hall and noticed the janitor cleaning the restroom. She had her cart outside the restroom while she was cleaning. I took a look at her cart hoping she would have left her keys, and luckily she did. I quickly and quietly grabbed her keys from her cart and headed back to the counselor's office.

I stood at the door with my hands shaking. I tried the first key and it didn't work. I tried the second key and that didn't work ether. I accidently dropped the keys on the floor. I looked around to see if anyone was near. I tried the third key and it worked, the doors opened. I walked straight to the back office. The first folder I opened was Thomas's. I jumped as I heard the door open. "What is this place?" Nikki asked.

"Uh, what are you guys doing here? Is anyone else with you?" I asked as I looked around the office.

"No, we came here to talk to a counselor. What are you watching?" Nikki asked.

I closed Thomas's folder and placed it back in the cabinets.

"I shouldn't be here, we should leave before someone see's us," I said.

"Wait, but what is this place?" Nikko asked.

"It's nothing... Shouldn't you two be looking for a counselor?" I asked.

"We're not leaving until you let us know," Nikki said.

Sigh, I grabbed the closes folder to me. I opened the folder and the TV turns on.

"Wait isn't that...." Nikki began to say.

"If you think you know her, you probably do. These files contain each student's future on earth," I stated.

"What, this isn't possible..." Nikki said.

"It's all right here," I handed Nikki the folder for prove.

"Just, you guys... please don't open your mouth about this place before we all get trouble," I said.

"Oh we know, we don't want to end up like most of your friends after the guys in white suits got to them," Nikki said.

"So you believe it too?" I asked.

"Of course, and hello... we are in psychology class with you learning about human behavior," Nikki replied.

"Well it looks like that's only one problem here at this school," I said.

Nikko runs over to the desk and shuts the open folder. Nikko opens another folder. "If this shows the future, I wonder if it'll show the past as well," she said.

I threw Nikko the remote, "Only one way to find out."

Nikko opens her folder and rewinds the screen to her past. She rewinds further back enough to see who her parents were, before they passed away.

"That's our father?" Nikki smiled as she watches her father on screen.

"But what happened, I need to see," Nikko said.

Nikki grabs the remote from Nikko, "Wait Nikko, do you really want to do this?"

"Yes, I do...I need to know," Nikko replied then snatched the remote out of Nikki's hands. Nikko plays a recording of her mother and father training at this school. We watched as her mother and father made it to the 3rd floor of trainer. During the graduation ceremony things got ugly. Nikko and Nikki's parents were running down the halls as the guys in the white suits were running after them. Their parents held hands and took one long kiss after a not having anywhere else to run. The guys in suits grabbed them and brought them to a room with hospital beds. "Help... they are trying to drug me, someone help!" Their mother screams. The guys in suits strap their mother down to restrain her. "No, don't hurt her!" their father screams. We watched as the guys in white suits shove pills down each of their mouth using a long tube.

Nikki turns the TV off, "I can't watch any more of this."

We stood there in silence. "I'm so sorry," I said.

Nikko bales her fist and looks around for something to punch.

Nikki breaks down and falls to the ground. "I can't even scream, I can't even scream," she repeated. Nikko runs out the room, I followed behind her.

"Wait, Nikko please don't go doing anything irrational please," I said.

"They killed my parents Angel, they killed my fucking parents!" Nikko said.

I held on to her tight as she cried in my arms. Nikki comes over and hugs her sister. I gave them their moment. "I know you guys don't want to hear this...but going out there, looking for justice isn't going to get you anywhere... not here. What we need to do is come up with a plan, to destroy this school and return to planet earth," I said.

The bell rings. "We have to leave, now..." I said. I grabbed a hand full of tissue for the girls to wipe their eyes. "You two have to be strong so we can really get justice for your parents," I said. We ran out the counselor's office before anyone could see us.

The rest of the night we stayed up in our dorm room thinking of a master plan. In the middle of planning, Nikki jumps out and walks away.

"Nikki, where are you going?" Nikko asked.

"We can't do this… we are just going to end up…" Nikki burst into tears.

Nikko walks over to Nikki and starts hugging her.

"Nikki we can't just sit here and do nothing," Nikko said.

"But there's like twenty of them and 3 of us, that doesn't even sound logical," Nikki said.

"She's right…" I interrupted. "We are going to need help, but I think I can gather up some people after they see what their future will look like if they stay here," I said.

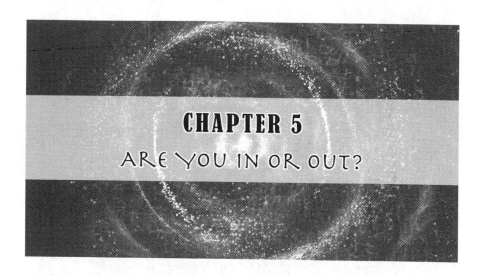

CHAPTER 5
ARE YOU IN OR OUT?

I KNOW IT WAS hard for Nikki and Nikko but they tried their best to keep their composer. Every morning we woke up to get an early morning workout. After our workout, we trained fighting in martial arts. "What happened to the other people you said you were going to get? Shouldn't they be training with us?" Nikki asked. "Don't worry, I'm going to talk to each of them," I replied. "Do that, and fast because I'm losing my patients and we are heading to the 3rd floor soon," Nikki replied.

In mathematics class I took notes of the names of my classmates. "Students, you're draft for this project is due soon so I hope everyone is taking full advantage of it. Once you make it to the 3rd floor, that's it... there's no turning back," Mr. Jamison announced. Mr. Jamison walks towards me. I quickly opened my notes and took out my fake money. "How are things going Angel?" he asked.

"Great, so far I have spent 30,000 and I projected to make 3 times that profit in less than 3 months," I said. "Perfect, keep up the good work," He replied. As soon as he walked away I continued with my list of each classmate.

It was lunch time; I needed a big meal to keep me functional. I ate my lunch and gather a list of names of people in the cafeteria. Thomas sat next to me, "Why does it feel like I haven't spoken to you in forever?" he asked.

"Maybe because we've both been so busy," I replied.

"Busy, or are you avoiding me?"

"Why would I avoid you?"

"That's what I'm trying to figure out... What are you working on over there?"

I hid my paper, "Nothing."

"So you are hiding something?"

"I'm not hiding something it's my project and I'm not ready to show people yet."

"Yea... okay, how's psychology going?

"Good, I'm just gathering up all the information I can."

Nikki and Nikko take a seat on next to me.

Thomas is surprised we are all eating lunch together. Thomas starts to whisper to me, "Since when did you and the twins hang out?"

"Something wrong?" Nikko interrupted.

"No... I just didn't know you all were so close," he replied.

"We are, is that a problem?" Nikki asked in defense.

Thomas looked for a reaction from me but I continued to eat my lunch.

Thomas gets up, "Okay, well I guess I'll catch up with you later."

"I don't know why you still hang out with him," Nikki said.

"What do you mean, Thomas is one of my closest friends," I replied.

"That doesn't believe in anything you say. You can't trust him," Nikki said.

"Why do you say that?" I asked.

"He's obviously a product of his environment, he will fall right in the cracks with the rest of them here," Nikki said.

"So what's new?" Nikko asked.

I showed her the list of people I've wrote down. We discussed the list over lunch then headed to Psychology class.

"Students as soon as you take your seat you may begin your test," Mrs. Jenkins announced to the class. "Test?" I questioned. "Yes, you didn't know...I wrote it on the board last week. You need to pay more attention Angel," She said.

I took my seat and looked at the test. I wrote my name down then started reading the questions. I didn't know the answers to any of these questions. I couldn't afford a bad grade in this class. I tapped my finger on the desk. I tried to open my bag and find the answers in my notes. I accidently dropped my bag. Mrs. Jenkins walks over to see what's going on. I tried to put my belongings back as fast as possible. "Is everything okay?" Mrs. Jenkins asked. Nikko rushes over to Mrs. Jenkins.

"Mrs. Jenkins, sorry…I have a question about question four," Nikko said.

"Yes, what is it?" Mrs. Jenkins asked.

Mrs. Jenkins turns around to help Nikko. Nikko leaves her paper open, with the answers written on the back. I copied down the answers as fast as I could.

"Now, go back to your desk and finish your test," Mrs. Jenkins said after answering her question. Mrs. Jenkins turns back around to face me. "Now, Angel, is everything okay?" She asked.

"Yes ma'am, sorry I was just looking for another pencil because mine was dull," I replied.

Mrs. Jenkins hands me a pencil, "All you had to do was ask."

"Thank you, Mrs. Jenkins."

After class I headed to the counselors office. As usual, the janitor was cleaning the restroom with her keys left on her cart. I took the list of names and opened each of their folders. I wrote down notes on each person and crossed out a couple names. I wrote as fast as I could then left the counselors office before anyone would notice me. I returned the keys to the janitors cart and headed to dinner. I looked over at Nikki and nodded by head. Nikko walks past me. I handed her a list of people name's and continued walking, leaving the cafeteria.

The first person on my list was Brianna Simmons. Brianna was studying to become a fashion designer. I found Brianna in the arts department, sewing a bag.

"Brianna… hi, could I speak to you?"

Brianna looses focus and accidently sews her shirt to the bag. I tried not to laugh.

The instructor runs over to Brianna, "Oh dear not again."

I asked Brianna to step outside the classroom with me.

"Do I know you from somewhere?" She asked.

"No, you don't but I just wanted to sit down with you and talk if that's okay?"

Brianna is hesitant to answer.

"Don't worry…. It'll definitely be worth your while," I said.

I walked with Brianna to the library. Nikki was already there with Carlos Martinez and Mellissa Singh. Carlos was training to be a pro baseball player. Mellissa was studying to be a FBI special agent.

Nikki stales everyone while I went to gather the rest of the names on the list. I found Julia Parker in the medical building. Julia's file truly traumatized me. Julia was studying to become a doctor but doesn't pass and has to take the course over until she does. Julia doesn't return to earth until she is forty. By that time, Julia mother has passed away. I didn't explain much to Julia. I just told her it would help her with her medical school and she was willing to come along with me. We then met up with Lindsey Bowman. Lindsey was studying for information technology. I found out she only studied this course because her parents forced her. In the future, Lindsey fails the class more than once and is force to return to earth. Lindsey becomes a homeless woman begging for money on the streets to survive.

I took the girls with the rest of the group to the library. When we arrived, Nikko was there with Kamen Johnson and Kelsey White. Kamen never wanted to come to this school and didn't care for it. Kelsey was studying to become a dentist. She was the oldest one here, in her early twenties. She had a daughter and husband on earth waiting for her to return.

"So is everyone here?" Nikki asked.

"No, we are missing one more person… I'll be back," I said.

Knock, Knock, "It's Angel."

Jocelyn opens the door. "Angel, what are you doing on this side of town?" Jocelyn asked.

"Nice room you got here," I said.

"You think so, my roommates aren't too bad ether," She said.

I didn't know how to get my words out to Jocelyn.

"What's going on?" She asked.

"Look, I need your help," I replied.

"Say no more." Jocelyn said without question.

Jocelyn and I entered the library. "So, now...is this everyone?" Nikki asked.

Jocleyn and I took our seats.

"Yes, this is everyone," I replied.

"So has anyone here every thought about what their future will be like after they leave this universe? I asked.

"Of course, I think I can speak for all of us when I say that," Carlos said.

"And everyone see's themselves having a bright future correct?" I asked.

"What's up with the obvious questions...I mean of course, we only enrolled in the school to secure a bright future," Carlos replied.

"What if I told you that you're future wasn't so bright, and that this school isn't going to help you but only harm you?" I asked.

Everyone looks at each other, waiting for someone to speak.

Nikko says, "Let's just cut to the chase, you guys are here because this school is basically going to ruin your life. We have brought you here for a second chance at life by destroying this school and returning to planet Earth."

"What, what do you mean second chance?" Kelsey asked.

"Some of you aren't going to pass the course while the other half of you is going to get involved in tragic events. Either way, it doesn't end to a bright future," Nikki said.

Julia speaks out, "Well I know I'm going to pass so I have nothing to worry about."

Nikki starts coughing trying to hint at Julia. "I am going to pass right?" She asked.

"No, Julia you don't pass the course and you don't return to earth until you're fifty," I said. "Fi- fifty, oh there's no way. How do you know this?" She asked.

"Now we can show you all prove but you have to promise not to say anything to anyone about it," I said.

We walked the group to the counselor's office and headed straight to the back.

"What is this place?" Mellissa asked.

"Mellissa, why don't you grab your folder over there to find out," I replied.

Mellissa looks for her name and grabs her folder.

"Okay, this is me…"

CHAPTER 6
MELLISSA'S FUTURE

I COULDN'T STAND BEING in the office for this long. I wanted to be on the streets fighting crime not filing papers. It's been a year since I've been working for the FBI. I joined Atlas Institution at 17 years old and I'm 28 now. Training for the FBI was no joke.

A group of police officers walked in the office. "Hey, hey... did you get my coffee like I wanted?" Ted (A police officer) asked. Every one of them began to laugh. "Ha, ha, so funny... get your own coffee while you're sitting on your ass in the passenger seat," I replied. "Oh Mellissa come on, you know I was joking," Ted replied. "Yea, we all know you're going to get that promotion soon, don't worry," Jonny, another police officer replied while patting me on the back. "Yea, yea... you guys say that last month," I replied. "It takes time Mellissa, you know that," Ted said.

The dispatcher sounds, "We have a code 249 on olive road, code 249." "That's us, let's move boys," Ted said. I watched as the police officers ran out the office. Seconds later and the FBI agents were running out the door. "I need you to look into these files, asap," My boss ordered. "Yes sir, I'm on it," I replied. I started gathering all the information on the suspect, Brendon Hall.

I didn't leave the office until 10pm. My apartment was just the way I left it of course because I'm by myself. After Atlas, I jumped start into my career. Once I got my foot in the door I didn't really have much time to meet anyone. Beer became my best friend after not being able to sleep at night. I thought about getting a puppy but I instead brought a cat because a dog would be too much work when you're never home.

I woke up the next morning with positive vibes after all the information I was able to gather up on Brendon Hall. I wore my favorite red suit with my red bottom heels. I walked in the office. Everyone was turning their heads because I usually don't dress up like this. I took my seat at my desk and quickly organized my files. My boss starts walking in my direction. "Show me what you got," He said. "Alright, everything Mr.Hall has done in the past is right here and also, everything he is planning to do is right here," I stated. "Planning, how do you know what he's planning?" he asked. Eh, he was dumb enough to post everything on his social media with the location," I replied. "They just never learn do they," He replied.

"Alright guys, we got ourselves a location," My boss said. "On it boss, you guys know the drill," Ted shouted. "Before you go, I thought I could tag along on this one," I said nervously. "Uh, not so fast Mellissa… it's not going to be that easy," My boss replied. I got up and chased him down. "With all due respect, nothing here has been easy and I just want to tag a long," I replied. "Yup, heard it before," He replied while racing towards the doors with the open file in his hand. He opens the door and hands me back the file on Brendon Hall, "Keep up the good work," He replied then left the office.

I slumped down at my desk and waited for a phone call, dispatch call or anything about the case. Twenty minutes pass by and everyone was gathering back in the office. "We'll get em next time," Jonny said. My boss walked in and headed straight to his office. No one was telling me what happened and why they were back so early. Five minutes later my boss is standing outside his door. "Melissa, my office," He said.

I got up and walked to his office. I was still confident because I believed I didn't do anything wrong. I found the victims location and all his information so there was no way I did anything wrong. "You gave us the wrong location," He said. "What do you mean, that's the address that was on his profile," I replied. "That's the address he was at, not… where he was going," He stated. "You always need to be one step ahead Mellissa," He continued. I was distraught at my mistake I was barley listening to him. I didn't purposely zone out and I hoped he didn't notice I wasn't listening. "You have great potential Mellissa, but there's still a lot of room for improving," he said.

My only goal at work now, was to make up for my mistake. I didn't want to disappoint everyone that believed in me here. I continued to stay positive. I even got asked on a date on the way home. The guy was okay, but work was my only priority right now.

Five months has past and they were still on the same case. I wanted to help anyway that I could but my boss wasn't trying to hear it. Instead, I just watched over his social media page to be a step ahead of his next move. I wanted to redeem myself and close this case for good.

Leaving work on a Friday night and just heading home was getting very old. I needed a different atmosphere for once. I went to a small pub not too far from my job. I sat down and immediately opened my laptop. "Doing work on a Friday night?" the bartender asked as he put my shot glass down. I quickly took the shot. "I know, I know... I shouldn't be working what is wrong with me," I said as I closed my laptop. "Hey, it's a Friday night... you're at a bar for crying out loud... enjoy your time and forget about work for the night," The bartender said as he put another shot on the table. "I didn't ask for another shot," I replied. "That one, is on me," he said. I wasn't hesitant to take the shot.

The bartender left to attend his guest. My mind was only focused on this case. I peeked my laptop open then shut it back. I couldn't help but to be curios to find out what Mr. Hall was up to. I knew I shouldn't look but I did. Mr. Hall social media contained videos of him and his friends with a bunch of pills and other drugs. Mr. Hall even had a video of him stating he was going to make a very important "lick" tonight. I didn't know what that meant but I was guessing it was bad based on the aggression in his voice.

I took a picture of his location then quickly closed my laptop. The bartender runs over to me, "Another shot for you?" he asked. "No, I'm actually going to head out," I replied. "Really, this early?" he asked. "Yea, I'm just not feeling too well I need some rest," I lied. I put his money on the table. "Alright, get home safe," he replied.

I couldn't waste anymore time. I got in my car and headed to the suspects destination. I turned off my headlights while arriving to the location. There was a large black van outside of a big house. I parked my car and grabbed my gun. I took off my heels and put on my sneakers. I ran outside to take my post at the side of the house. Before making my move on the suspects I called for backup. I searched around the house to see where the guys were. The lights were on upstairs. I quietly opened the door and made my way up stairs.

I peeked through the door and there was the suspect with an accomplice stealing from this house. "Freeze!" I yelled with my gun pointing at the suspects. The suspect accomplice drops the stolen good out his hand. "On the ground!" I yelled. The accomplice kneels to the floor while Brendon stood there looking for an escape. "There's no way out. Drop the stuff and get on the floor!" I yelled. Brendon drops the stolen good and jumps out the window.

I heard police sirens as I ran down stairs. I watched as Brendon struggles to stand up. I ran out to the front door and lost his sight. I held my gun up while looking for him. My heart is pounding as the sirens sound louder and louder. I felt his presence around me. I looked over my back several times. THUMP! Brendon runs up to me and hits me in the back of the head. We wrestle around for my gun. I used what I learned to throw him to the ground but my gun flew away while doing so. I ran to grab my gun while he was on the floor. I turned around and Brendon hits me in the face with a glass bottle. I couldn't feel my face as I hit the ground. All I knew is that I fell face first and may have lost a couple teeth from it. I was in pain but I could barley feel it. I was light headed. I watched Brendon walk towards me and points the gun towards me. I then heard, "Put the gun down Mr. Hall!" from a police officer. I couldn't remember anything after that. I passed out.

I woke up in a hospital bed. There were balloons, flowers and cards all over the room. Ted and Jonny walk in with some more flowers. "Well, look who's awake," Ted said as he rushes to give me a hug. "Uh, what happened? How long have a been here?" I asked. "Not too long, Ted is still riding passenger seat," Jonny said. I laugh. "Did you guys get Brendon Hall?" I asked. "We did, we did," Ted replied. "Oh, yes… finally," I replied. "Now that, that's over I'm ready to head home," I said as I try to get up from my bed. "Oh no, don't… stay here and heal Mellissa," Jonny said. "Uh, I think I've healed enough I feel fine," I replied. I squirmed to get out my bed. Jonny and Ted put their head down and I used all my might to get out the bed. "What is going on, am I hyped up on medicine or what because it's hard for me to get out of this bed…" I said. I quickly pulled the covers off my body. One of my legs was gone.

I screamed for dear life. Ted and Jonny held on to me while I cried my eyes out. "How, how did this happen!" I yelled. "Well once you were on the ground Brendon Hall had the gun pointed at you. We yelled at him not surrender but he wouldn't. He shot you in the leg right before we were able to get him," Ted explained. My head started feeling light headed. The nurses run in the room. Everyone kept talking to me at once. "Just Stop, Stop!" I yelled.

"Stop, Stop! I'm done… I don't want to see anymore," Mellissa closed her folder. She starts feeling on her legs. Brianna starts patting her on the back and tears start falling down her eyes. "Well, now that you know…. You can just prevent that incident from happening," Brianna said. "That's not even it. Something like that can happen at any moment," Mellissa replied. "But didn't you know that when you signed up?" Carlos asked. I couldn't believe he said that. "Well, it's true…" Carlos repeated. "I guess I didn't really think that much about it… but seeing it happen in front of my eyes is a different story. I don't know if I'm ready for that," Mellissa said. "But I already made a decision…. What am I going to do?" Mellissa questions. "We're in this together Mellissa," I replied. "This is why we need to destroy this institution," Nikki said. "I don't know…" Kelsey replied. Nikko steps in, in anger. "Did you not just see what happened?" Nikko asked. "Yea… but," Kelsey said. Nikko stops her. "You know what, I'm not even trying to hear it… let's just take a look at your file Kelsey. Instead of just your future, let's look at your past too," Nikko replied.

CHAPTER 7
KELSEY'S FUTURE

"Mommy you're going to work?" My daughter asked me while tugging on my pants. I was doing last minute packing for *Atlas Institution* and I couldn't be more excited to be back on track with school. After high school my fiancé went into the military while I stayed home with our new born baby. My fiancé made sure we had everything we needed in order to be secure. I started to feel restless from being in the house all day and all night. I wanted to be a provider for daughter just like my fiancé was. I wanted more for my life than just being a house wife.

My mother is the one who told me about *Atlas Institution*. She is the one who suggested I should go while she watches over my daughter for me. I had a bitter sweet feeling as I'm packing my bags. My daughter is three years old now. I finished packing my suitcase. "I don't know about this," I said. "Don't worry, by the time you're back it'll be like you never left," My mother replied. "How long do you think I'll be there?" I asked. "Not long at all. I doubt you'll even be there for a whole year," She replied.

I looked over to my daughter playing dress up with her dolls. "Look, see is going to work too," My daughter said. I laughed while trying to hold back my tears. "I love you Braylee," I said while holding on to her tightly. "I love you mommy," She replied. I grabbed my suitcase and headed to the door.

*fast forward to Atlas Institution

Being away from my daughter is very hard but it's also motivating. I was studying to become a dentist but didn't know it would be this complicated. I just finished my quiz for anatomy. Next week the teacher was giving us a wax quiz. I spent the majority of my time studying. I missed my family so much. I kept imaging what they're doing at the moment. I also wondered if my fiancé was home or not.

The third floor training was intense. Today in class we were actually going to be shadowing some real dentist to get hands on training. I was so excited to be almost done with school. I couldn't believe graduation day was right around the corner. My grades were decent enough to pass and I really just wanted to be back on planet earth already.

I walked in the classroom and the teacher has papers on each person's desk. When I took my seat I realized the papers on my desk were my failing grades. "Students, as you know we are getting closer and closer to gradation, I know you all are excited," My teacher announced. "But before you leave my class I need you to complete one more assignment to let me know if you guys are truly ready for the real world of dentistry," He said. "On your desk is every failing grade or "barley passing" grade you've made since you enrolled in this school. You're assignment today is to turn every failing grade into a passing one. The assignment starts now," My teacher annouced.

I had 10 failed papers on my desk. I quickly started each quiz one by one. "How long do we have to finish this?" One of my classmates asked. "Until the end of the class period," My teacher replied. "But... what if we don't finish," My classmate replied. My teacher chuckled. "What do you think you're going to say to a child's mother when you have to finish working on their teeth and you have 3 other clients waiting in the waiting room? Are you going to say you aren't going to be able to finish, or are you going to get the job done?" My teacher asked. "Get the job done," My classmate replied.

I tried to not let my nerves get the best of me. So far I've completely 6 quizzes and I was for sure they would all be passing grades. I couldn't remember everything from the other quizzes. Some stuff I didn't even bother looking over after I failed the first time. The bell rang and I was still working on my quiz. "Alright students, time's up," my teacher said. As everyone got up to turn in their papers I stayed in my seat to finish.

Once the line started getting short I ran to the back of the line. I turned my papers in. "Hey, that's a big ring you got there... You're married?" My teacher asked. "Engaged actually, my fiancé said we could get married as soon as I return back to earth," I said. "Isn't that sweet, congrats to you both." My teacher replied.

I came to class the next day praying I passed the assignment. I took my seat and nervously waited for the teacher. "Students the assignment is being graded as we speak, but for now we are going to partner up and study while I get some grading done," The teacher announced. My classmate Jessie and I looked at each other as soon as he said "partner up". I took a seat next to her. "How's it going girl?" I asked. "It's going... I'm just nervous about that assignment that's all," Jessie replied. "Me too, but we'll be fine," I replied. "I sure do hope so, because you know what happens when you fail?" She asked. "What happens?" I replied. "You have to start the whole course all over again," She replied. My jaw dropped. "Why didn't anyone tell me this?" I asked. "They say it periodically, not as much as they should because they don't want to scare people," She replied.

Jessie and I opened our books and started studying. While studying we kept coming back to the same conversation. "I just can't believe it... but we have nothing to worry about," I said. Jessie dropped her pencil and took a big sigh. "I have a daughter Kelsey, I can't afford to fail," Jessie said. I looked at her and smiled. "I have a daughter too Jessie, and we are going to return back home to them, don't worry," I replied.

Our teacher had us studying for 3 days straight while he graded our papers. I wondered how much failing grades my classmates had. Today in class we took our seats and waiting for instruction. "Okay, students... I have finally finished grading your assignments. I took my time on each and everyone one of your assignments to make sure I know who is really ready to graduate," My teacher explained.

My teacher gathers up false teeth on his desk. "Now, I am still a children's dentist at heart so excuse me for my creativity but as you see here I have false teeth on my desk. I'm going to hand everyone false teeth and you are going to lift up the tongue. Under the tongue there will be a piece of paper stated if you failed or passed the course," My teacher explained while hanging out the false teeth. "Once you get your teeth you are excused for the day," He said.

I nervously waited for him to make his way to me but he kept passing me. I couldn't take the anticipation. I watched as Jessie received her false teeth. I watched her lift up the tongue because she obviously couldn't wait. She started screaming for joy. "Jesse, please," My teacher said. "I'm sorry, I'm sorry…. I'm coming home Molly!" Jessie said as she skipped out the class room. I couldn't be happier for her.

I was one of the last people to receive my false teeth. I grabbed my back pack and waited to open it in the hallway. I lifted up the tongue and the piece of paper had the words "Failed" on it. I couldn't be more devastated. I was speechless. I dropped to the floor and cried. I looked at my engagement ring and started crying even harder. I cried all the way to my room.

I heard knocking on my door, it was Jesse. "Oh no, don't tell me," She said as I opened the door. "This is it, I failed… my life is over," I cried. "Kelsey stop, you have to stay strong at this point," Jessie said. I started to get angry. "Be strong, how do you expect me to be strong at a time like this?" I asked. "Because… I know, it's going to be hard but listen Kelsey, you have to stay strong so you can pass this course and make it back home," Jessie replied.

I started pacing around the room. "What the fuck, what the fuck, what the fuck!" I yelled. "Calm down," Jessie replied. "Don't tell me to calm down when you're going back to earth and I have to sit here and live with the fact that my daughter is just getting older and I'm missing her life. I'm missing my daughter's life!" I yelled. Jessie starts rubbing my back. I couldn't stop crying.

When gradation day came around I was being sent back to the first floor with some other people that didn't pass. I was assigned the same teacher and doing the same assignments. I found myself crying a lot and feeling hopeless. Having to complete training again was dreadful.

After I completely the first floor I wasn't headed back to the 2nd floor training. My teachers face couldn't be more disappointed to see me. I told her all the stories about my future plans and how dedicated I was to seeing my daughter again. Seeing my old teachers face's made me feel even worse. As the days went by I started skipping my classes. I found myself sitting in the bathroom a lot just crying and reminiscing on my days back on earth. I was depressed and felt like a terrible mother.

Once I was finally back on the third floor I felt a little better. It was hard for me to focus but I managed to get the job done. I didn't talk to anyone and just did my work. The day my teacher pulled out his false teeth was going to be the end of it all for me. I was finally going to return back to earth with my family. As soon as he handed me my false teeth I ran out the door.

"Okay stop, I am done with all these surprises, did I pass or not?" Kelsey asked. "No, you didn't pass," I replied. Kelsey leaned against the table to keep her balance from falling. "I didn't pass, but that was my second time. What happened... how could this Happen..." Kelsey asked. "As you can see you became depressed and really just stopped trying," I replied. "But my daughter... my family..." Kelsey began to say.

"Well, what I can say is you did actually pass the third time around," I said. "Oh Thank God," Kelsey said. "Would you like to see more?" I asked. "Oh nope, I'm good because that is definitely not going to be my future," Kelsey replied.

CHAPTER 8
CARLOS FUTURE

"HEY LOOK, I FOUND my file. Looks like I'm up next," Carlos said as he opens his file.

"Just fast forward until I'm hitting homeruns on the field," Carlos said. Nikko pressed play after hearing moaning sounds. Carlos was in the bed with a female. "Hey, well…. maybe we can start here," Carlos said.

I took another girl home from the club. This one was unexpected though because she wasn't giving me any attention the whole night. The sex wasn't all that good so I kind of wish I didn't invite her to my place afterwards. I put on my clothes and watched her start to fall asleep in my bed. "Come on girl, you gotta wake up. You want me to call you a ride?" I asked. "No, I'm tired I can't move," She replied. "Oh no, come on… you gotta wake up," I said as I'm taping her on the shoulder. This was the awkward part. I just went ahead and called the uber ride. "You're ride arrives in 4 minutes," I said. "Okay, where's my shoes?" she asked. "I don't know…" I replied. I looked around for everything that was hers. "Alright, one minute…." I said as I'm lifting her out my bed. "Come on, you awake?" I asked. She already fell asleep and the uber driver just arrived.

I quickly picked her up like a baby and carried her outside. "Ride for Carlos?" the uber driver asked. "Yup, that's me…" I said as I put the seat belt on this girl. "She okay?" the uber driver asked. "Yea man, she's good… I just had to make sure she is strapped up and ready to go," I replied. "Alright man, you have a good night," The uber driver said. "You too man," I replied then shut the door.

I ordered pizza and started watching TV but nothing entertaining was on. I turned my lights off and went through my phone. I then found myself watching porn as if I didn't just have sex. The sex was wack anyway so I had to make up for it by watching my favorite porn star work her magic.

I only got 3 hours of sleep. I woke up and rushed in the shower to get ready for work. I drew my line in the morning and took off in my motorcycle. "Hey, good morning Carlos!" My coworker, Andy said. "Yea....." I replied. I went behind the bar and made some coffee. "Long night?" Andy asked. "Too long. Should have never took that girl home," I replied. "Hey, you got to have some self control buddy," Andy replied. "Yea, yea," I wasn't trying to hear the same speech Andy always gives me.

"Everyone, this is our new hire Alyssa," My boss said. Alyssa was beautiful and curvy with short born hair and red lip stick. "Nice to meet you Alyssa."

"Like wise... and your name is?" She asked.

"Carlos," I replied.

"Nice to meet you Carlos," She said.

I watched Alyssa and my boss walk to the back kitchen. "Don't even think about it," Andy said. "Think about what.... I'm just checking out the new girl. I'm trying to see if she's good for this company," I said. "Yea buddy, I think that's the mangers job," Andy replied.

I was working another double shift today. I didn't mind because the night crowd had the best tips. My boss left before sun down. That means that I was now in charge. Another manager did come but he was a push over and I basically ran the place.

By 8pm the restaurant was packed. I stopped taking tables around this time and only helped my bar guest. "Another shot for my girl Carlos!" My guests were practically screaming at me for drinks. They were cute though, and I could tell the only wanted my attention. "Uh hi, can I ask you something?" Alyssa walked behind the bar and asked. "Go for it," I said as I'm doing a million things at once. "Sorry to bother you, but I customer that has a discount card and I don't know how to use it," She replied. I smiled at the frustration on her face. "You have the card with you?" I asked. Alyssa hands me the discount card. I passed my customers their drinks then ran to the computers. "See, all you have to do is click on the table number then swipe the card... easy," I demonstrated. "Oh, wow... sorry to bother you I didn't know it was going to be that easy and I was freaking out a little," She replied. "I could tell by the look on your face, don't stress its easy money," I replied.

The night flew by faster than I expected. The girls flirting with me at the bar were my last customers. "Psss, Carlos," One of the girls flagged me down. "Wassup ladies, ready for the check?" I asked. She then whispers in my ear, "Grab the check but also... put your number on it for my friend over here." I smiled and laughed.

As I'm walking over to the computers I noticed Alyssa counting her tips for the night. "Made a some good money tonight?" I asked. "Yea... not too bad being that I'm new I guess," She replied. "Yea, it'll get better," I said. I printed out the check for my customers. I felt them staring at me while I was doing so. I only had a couple seconds to decide if I wanted to give this girl my number and possibly take her home tonight.

"Here you go ladies, and you have a great night," I said as I put the check down. I didn't give them my number and I didn't want to face the awkwardness so I headed to the back kitchen. Alyssa walks in right after me. "Hey, did you make those girls upset or something?" She asked. "NO, why?" I asked. "I don't know, they just seemed upset. They're gone now though," She stated. "Woo, good," I chanted. The guys in the kitchen laughed at me. "Ayye man, this is the first time I see you turn down a girl," The chef said. Alyssa was walking away by this time but I was still afraid she heard his comment. "Yea man, I'm turning on a new leaf," I whispered. They all started laughing because they didn't believe me.

"Cheers to your first day," I said to Alyssa as I handed her a shot. "Really, are we supposed to be doing this?" She asked. "Hey, I'm the real boss around here don't forget that," I said. She started laughing. We each took a shot. I grabbed my broom to start cleaning but got distracted by the baseball game on TV. "Let's go baby, let's go!" I yelled. My favorite player was running for homerun. "You got this, let's go!" I yelled. He made it to home run a slight second before the opposite opponent with the ball did. "He's safe, I know he's safe!" I yelled. "I don't know, seemed pretty close to me it's hard to tell," Alyssa replied. "No, I saw exactly what happened... he's safe," I replied. "He's safe!" I chanted as the game ended and my favorite team won the game. "I'm guessing you're a big baseball fan huh?" Alyssa asked. "You have no idea. "There was a point in my life when baseball was life. That's all that I cared about.... All I wanted to do, it was everything to me," I told as I'm cleaning my bar. "So what happened?" Alyssa asked. "Well after training, the only thing I wanted was to be drafted by my favorite team but they never picked me up. Only team that wanted me was the worst team in history!" I explained. "Oh, they couldn't have been that bad?" She asked. "Okay, they weren't that bad but my heart was set on this team. It was a dream of mine to play for the dodgers and playing for another team would just crush me. So that's when I decided to move to LA and try out as a walk on but plans didn't work out that way. I had LA bills to pay and I was just getting older you know, so I ended up getting a job here. I've been here for 3 years now," I explained. "Wow, so what's your plan now?" Alyssa asked. "Shoot, when you find out you let me know because I have no idea myself," I replied.

After cleaning and closing down the register I knew this was the perfect time for me to ask Alyssa over to my house. "So what brought you to LA, Alyssa?" I asked to start conversation. "Writing, I want to be a television writer," She replied. "Wooo, that's a tough field to go into with a lot of rejection you have to face," I replied. "Yea, I know... it's a tough field to go into but I'm never going to stop trying because I know that's what I want to do for the rest of my life. I'd be too depressed without so I have to give it my all," Alyssa replied.

We grabbed our belongings and started heading out the door. "Alyssa, never give up on your dreams okay," I said. "Thanks Carlos, I won't," replied. "Alyssa!" I yelled out to her before she went too far. "You want to go out tonight? Maybe get a couple drinks over dinner?" I asked. "Uh, no I can't tonight... have to catch up on my writing. I gave myself a dead line for this new project I'm working on," She replied. "Oh, yea... that's great then, I'll see you at work," I replied.

After she left I looked through my server handbook. The girl from tonight left her number for me instead so I decided to give her a call. I quickly took a shower when I got home. I drew myself a couple lines while waiting for the girl to come over. As soon as my door bell rang I rushed to the door. "Hi, wow... did you change clothes?" I asked. The girl had on a skimpy red dress. "I did, I wanted to look cute for you," She replied. "Yea, you look great... come in and make yourself at home," I said. The girl walks in my house and immediately jumps on the bed. "I like the way you get comfortable," I said. I jumped on the bed after her and started kissing all over her neck. I then took off that red dress she had on.

While this girl and I were under the covers making out, we hear my door bell rang. "Probably, my neighbor... I'll let it ring," I said then continued to kiss her. We then heard banging on the door. "Open up Carlos, its Sabrina!" Sabrina yelled. Sabrina was a girl I've been hooking up with a couple years now. I could tell the girl I was with was getting nervous as she reached for her bra and underwear. "Don't worry, she's just a friend," I said. I put some shorts on and ran to the door.

"What's up Sabrina?" I asked. Sabrina burst through the doors. "Who's this?" She asked. "Oh, this is.... I'm sorry what was your name again?" I asked the girl I brought home. She didn't even bother to answer me and just continued putting her clothes on. "Anyway, I just wanted to show you this," Sabrina said while pulling out three pregnancy tests out her purse. "I'm pregnant, and the baby yours," Sabrina said. The girl I brought home ran out the door after she heard that.

"Good, glad she's gone... now we can really talk," Sabrina said. I took a seat on my bed to try to process this all. "So what are we going to do, do you want to move in here with me or...." I began to say.

"Um, definitely not Carlos... I want an abortion and I need you to pay for it," She said. "What! You can't be serious?! You're not even going to ask me how I feel about it?" I said. "There's no need, you can't afford a baby so there's no need for me to ask you," She replied. "Oh but I can afford the abortion, is that what you're saying?" I replied. "Look Carlos, no hard feeling but what are you doing with your life. You're pushing thirty and you're still bartending. I'm doing us both a favor here," Sabrina stated. "Killing my baby is not a favor and I'm not giving you the money," I said.

Sabrina stood there and looked at me for a while. "Look, I know things don't look good on my end but it'll get better," I said. "Better? How the hell will it get better Carlos? I really wish you would have just signed with that baseball team because then, we could have kept this baby and be ready financially," Sabrina said. "Well it's too late for that Sabrina isn't it! It's too late!" I yelled. "Right, and it's also too late for me to change my mind," Sabrina rushed to the door. "Never call me again," She said then ran out the door.

I was so angry I didn't know what to do with myself. I grabbed my bat and started swinging in the air as if I was hitting a baseball. "It's too late, that's what she said… it's too late for my fucking child's life!" I yelled. I held the bat in my hand firmly and started to build up anger before I knew it. I started hitting everything in my sight. "It's too late!" I yelled. I heard knocking on my door but I was already zoned out hitting everything in my sight and not caring what's so ever.

My Neighbors broke down the door. "Get away from me!" I yelled. "What's going on?" My neighbor screamed. I started hitting my windows. "It's too late, get away from me!" I yelled. The police barge their way inside. I hit one of them with the bat and the other one tackles me to the ground and hand cuffs me.

"Alright, alright, I get it…" Carlos said as he closes his folder. "You know I may seem like an asshole but I really always wanted a family, I can't watch the rest of this," He said.

CHAPTER 9
BRIANNA'S FUTURE

"ALRIGHT, BRIANNA YOU READY to see your future?" I asked. "I'm ready," Brianna replied. I opened Brianna's file.

The mall was packed as usual for a Friday evening. I went shopping on break to find an outfit for a shoot I had tomorrow. Everything was so expensive I really had to shop smart. I only had ten minutes left for my break and the line was extremely long. "Hey girl I'm opening the register in the men's department, you can come with me," my co-worker said.

My co worker starts ringing me up. "Going somewhere special?" She asked. "A photo shoot I have tomorrow. I'm styling this model," I replied. "So you didn't buy anything for yourself?" She asked. "Nope, can't afford it. Thanks for ringing me up fast I have to run and clock back in before they come looking for me," I replied.

I quickly ran to the break room to change my clothes. "Why do you always change your clothes?" my co worker asked. "Because, I don't want to look like I work here all the time," I replied. My manager rushed through the doors. "Brianna, are you back yet?" he asked. "Coming right now," I replied as I'm closing my locker.

My manager stood there and awkwardly waited for me. I clocked back in and he walked me to the sales floor. "We need you to watch the front for ten minutes," My manager tells me. "And who's recovering me?" I asked. "Chelsea is recovering you but she's running a little late," He replied as he walks me to the front of the store.

Standing in the front of the store felt like you were being punished. When standing in the front you are told to greet the customers and watch the door to prevent thefts. "Hi, can you help me with something? There's this dress I really love but I can't seem to find it," A customer explains. She shows me a picture in her phone of the dress. "Oh that dress is going to be to the right next to the registers," I told her. "Umm, well are you able to show me?" She asked. "Actually ma'am, I am not a loud to leave my post here but once you make it to the register I'm sure there's an associate there that can help you," I replied. The customer storms off upset but there was nothing I could do about it.

I stood there trying to keep my fake smile. It was fifteen minutes now and still no sign of Chelsea. My manger walks over to me and said, "So you are going to have to stay here for another thirty minutes because Chelsea isn't coming in today but Anthony will be here in thirty minutes to take your place." Anthony was the security guard they have ever so often. I couldn't dare stay here for the rest of my shift so I was happy to hear that he was coming in.

Time was going by so slow and so many thoughts about my life were running through my head. My life was being wasted away at this very spot when I could do so much more. Anthony showed up and I couldn't be happier to see him. "Woo, alright... the front is all yours," I joyfully said. I started walking to the register when my manager stopped me. "You're going to be in the fitting room for the rest of your shift," he tells me.

I walk in the fitting room in and there were a pile of clothes on the counter. There was a long line of guest waiting to get a fitting room. Customer's starts complaining as guest in the fitting room start walking out to show their friends their outfits. "Oh come on, we've been waiting," A customer shouted. "And I have been waiting too, and now it's my turn," The other customer replied. The demographics here are high end. That also meant that they felt more entitled when they really shouldn't.

"Excuse me, miss," a customer calls me to her fitting room. I walk over to her dressing room and she only had her bra and underwear on. It looked like she had some work down to her body and just wanted to show it off. "Can I get your opinion, I have this really important meeting I'm going to and I can't seem to decide on which top with these pants," She said. "Definitely this top with those pants, it'll make you look more professional and it's in season," I stated.

ATLAS

I began hanging the clothes on the counter as fast as I could. While I was hanging the clothes a customer dumps a pile of clothes on the counter. "Thank you," She said. I didn't bother to say anything back. Nothing she brought back had hangers so I went to look in her dressing room. When I got there it was a mess with clothes and hangers everywhere. "Great, just great," I said. "Excuse, can I try on these clothes," I customer yelled. "Just give me a second," I replied. I picked up all the clothes and told the customer next in line to take the room. "Please bring everything back on the hanger's ma'am," I said.

"Oh my gosh, you were so right about this top with these pants," A customer said as she looks in the mirror at her outfit. "You know, have you ever thought about being a stylist?" she asked. "Yea, that's actually the plan. To be a stylist and fashion designer," I replied. "Oh that's great, are you going to school for it or?" the customer asked. "I've already completed school actually and now it's all on me really to find clientele and build as a designer," I replied. "Yes you really should so you can leave this place. How do you even make a living working here?" She asked. "You don't... and that's short of my problem now. You need money to make money you know," I stated.

The customer walks out her room three minutes later and hands me the clothes she doesn't want. "Good luck with your fashion career," She said. "Thank you," I replied. "Oh, I left the other clothes in the room," she said while walking out. I walked in the room and she has clothes everywhere as if I was her maid and this was her house.

I was so relieved for the night to finally be over. I grabbed my stuff out my locker. I started heading to the door. "Hey, how you getting home?" My coworker, Dell asked. "Buss-ing it." I replied. "I'll take you home, you shouldn't be riding the bus this late," Dell replied. "Thanks Dell, I appreciate it," I replied.

Dell and I walk to her car across the street. "Why do you park over here?" I asked.

"Because I can't afford to park in the parking lot, its way too much money for what we're making," She replied. "Tell me about it, I can barely afford to eat at the food court," I said.

It was going to take Dell forty five minutes to get to my house. "I live so far, you don't have to do this. You can drop me off at my bus stop," I asked. "No girl don't worry I got you. I'm not like that. I know how it is you know. We got to help each other out because no one wants to end up at a damn clothing store for the rest of their lives. You know some people do that, just work retail and die. We can't live like that," She explained.

"You know I've been there for 2 years now when I was only planning on staying for six months," I told Dell. "Yea, what happened?" She asked. "They're trying to promote me to shift lead so I'm just waiting for that to be able to make the bills while I try to get my fashion career to take off," I explained. "Oh you do fashion, that's cool. You must get a lot of ideas at work huh?" Dell asked. "Yea, I guess... sometimes I'm just too busy working to even pay attention though," I replied.

Dell pulled into my apartment complex. "So who you live with?" she asked. "I have 2 roommates," I replied. "Oh, you got a three bedroom apartment. That looks pretty small," She replied. "Yea, it is because it's only a one bedroom. My two roommates share the room in the back and I have the living room," I said. "Oh wow, and I bet you're still paying a lot huh?" She asked. "Well with what I'm making yea, you can definitely say I'm paying a lot," I replied. "Thanks so much for the ride," I said as I gather my bags. "Of course, you let me know whenever you need something. I got you," Dell replied. I closed the door. Dell rolls the window down. "Hey, good luck on your shoot tomorrow, you got this," She yelled. "Thank you, drive home safe Dell!" I yelled.

The next day I was up early and ready for the shoot. I called an uber to take me to the location. The photographer and I met on a desert hill. I started putting my looks together while waiting for the model to arrive.

"Hello, sorry I'm late," the model said as she rushes out her car. "It's okay, are you ready to get started?" I asked. "Yup, all ready," she replied. I gave her the first look for this location. She wore a long colorful skirt with a crop top and combat boots. "I absolutely love this look," she said. "Alright, we all set to take some photos?" the photographer asked. "Oh yes, I am ready," The model said while admiring her outfit.

The photographer only took a couple shots to get "the one". After that, we were headed to our next location, the street.

"This is the street look I thought you would look great wearing," I said. "Oh, yes… I know this is going to look great," She replied. She quickly put on the outfit and we got started. After the 3rd and finale look the shoot was over. The model paid me the amount of $100 dollars and it only took 2 hours to get it.

The next day at work I got in line to return the clothes during my lunch. "Hey boo, these didn't work out for you?" My co worker Jose asked. "Nope, I thought they would but I think their meant for tall people only," I replied. "Girl, you could have put on some heels and call it a day," Jose replied. "I'm not a heel type of girl," I replied. Jose rolled his eyes. "Okay, well here you go… you are getting 150 back in cash," He said while handing me my refund. "Thank you Jose," I replied.

I noticed Dell in the break room. "Aye, how'd it go yesterday?" she asked.

"It went great," I replied.

"She paid you a lot?" Dell asked.

"100 dollars," I replied.

"Oh wow, you have to work like two shifts to make that here," Dell said. "You're on your lunch?" She asked.

"Yup," I replied.

"Oh, what you going to eat?" Dell asked.

"I don't know, I'll probably go get a banana down stairs or something," I replied. "Just a banana?" Dell questioned.

"Yea, I need to save this for my rent," I explained.

"Uh oh, no good," Dell said as she rushes to the fridge. "Look my mom made some beans and tortillas and corn and rice," She said. She puts the food in front of me. "Take it, I already ate," She said.

"Really? don't just say that to be nice to me," I said.

"Girl no.. I just ate I'm telling you, eat it," She replied. "I have to clock back in but that's yours eat it, you'll really like it," She said.

I sat down and ate Dell's food but I wasn't happy about it. The fact that I couldn't even afford to eat really bothered me. When my break was over I headed back to the sales floor. Today I was running clothes to floor and fixing the tables. It was a really busy day for us. I noticed my manger watching us employees on the floor. I ran the clothes to their original place as fast as I could. It was ten minutes before closing and I've been waiting to use the restroom for the longest. I was finally done fixing three tables and could now head to the restroom.

I looked at myself in the mirror. I was sweating so bad my makeup was coming off. I looked tired and not myself. I used the restroom and thought about life and how I didn't want to be here. I washed my hands then just stood there waiting for the store to close.

After the store was finally closed I went out the sales floor. Two out of three tables that I've fixed were completely messy once again. "I don't know why I even bother," I said. "What you mean?" Dell asked. "I literally just fixed both of these tables and now look at them, messy again" I said. "Yup, the customers don't be caring," Dell replied.

"Alright, everyone to the front," My manager announces. "Alright before we close I just want to inform you guys on how much we made. Men's department made 28,000 and Woman's made 58,000. So that's very good," My manager said. He starts clapping and we all clap with him. "Alright, so we are going to have a good closing shift tonight, please be sure to work as fast as you can so we can get out of here," My manager said.

*Pause

Nikko pauses the video. "Can we just fast forward this," Brianna asked. Nikko fast forwards the video and it showed Brianna doing the same thing every day. Going to work and going to sleep. The only time she had to style anyone was on her day off.

"Okay, there's no need for me to even continue watching this," Brianna said.

"Okay Julia, your next," I said while looking for her file. "Actually, I prefer not to see my future," Julia replied. "Okay, fine with me... that means your next, Lindsey," I said. "Yea, I'm with Julia on this one... I don't want to see my future," Lindsey replied. "Okay, Kamen... you're the last one," I said. "Play it. I need to see why my mother wanted me to come here so badly," Kamen said.

CHAPTER 10
KAMEN'S FUTURE

"Kamen Johnson... Kamen," Mrs. Bradley repeated. "Huh, yea?" I picked me head up from the best nap ever. Mrs. Bradley was always on my back about not sleeping in her class. "Kamen, how do you expect to pass if you sleep during class?" She asked. "But I'm passing Mrs. Bradley..." I replied. "Yea, and I'm not sure how you're doing that," Mrs. Bradley replied and returned to her desk.

I guess I was the only person here that hated this school. Everyone else was so excited for their future and their career when I still didn't know what I wanted to do with my life. The day they made us decide I was forced to answer so I said Engineer. Engineering had a wide range of class courses so I thought I couldn't do wrong with my decision.

While everyone spent their time studying and getting ready for finals I was in the gym. The gym was the only place I could have peace of mind. The best part about the gym on the 3rd floor was the pool. I could swim for hours and hours. I would even skip class sometimes to go swimming.

Only three days before graduation and I've never been more excited. I stood in line to receive my cap and gown. "Name?" The guy asked. "Kamen Johnson," I replied. I watched as he searched for my name. "Sorry no, Kamen Johnson on this list," he said. "What, that must be a mistake. Are these lines separate by alphabetical order?" I asked. "Nope, we all have the same list and your name isn't on it... sorry," he said.

"Kamen, may I have a word with you?" Maria asked. I'm guessing Maria would have some answers for me. She leads me to this office. I walked in and all of my teachers were there. "What's this about?" I asked. "Kamen, I have spoken with your teachers and they tell me you have a lack of enthusiasm for your career. They say you are skipping class and when you are in class you fall asleep. Is that correct?" Maria asked.

"Yes, that is… practically, but I do now I am passing all of my classes," I replied. "Unfortunately son, that's not going to be enough; please have a seat," Maria said.

I took a seat and stared at each one of my teachers in front of me. "You all are trying to prevent me from graduating, why? I asked them. "Kamen it's not that we are trying to prevent you from graduating we just want insure that you are prepared and ready for the real world," Mrs. Bradley said. "So what does this mean?" I asked. "Kamen, I am going to give you two choices here okay. The first one is taking the whole course over because we are not going to pass you this time around. The second choice is for you to work for us here at *Atlas Institution*," Maria explained. "So ether way I have to stay here?" I asked. "That is correct," Maria replied.

I sat there in the desk and tried to gather this all in my head. I hated having to think on the spot like this. "You all can be excused," Maria told my teachers. Maria waited for each of them to leave before speaking. "Kamen, let me tell you something… I know your teachers weren't very fond of you. I also know that they are jealous of you," Maria said.

"Jealous, how so?"

"You can sleep the whole class period but still make straight A's on quizzes. You have even skipped class but your scores are in the high percentile here. I know most of your teachers wish they were able to do that," Maria chuckles. "They envy your intelligence you have that takes no effort to excel," Maria explains.

"But if you know that, then why are you trying to fail me?" I asked.

"Oh dear I would never try to fail you. I want the best for you and that's why I want you to work for me."

"How would I work for you?"

"You ever notice those guys walking around in the white suits?"

"Yes."

"I want you to join them and be a part of my team here."

I didn't know what to say I was confused about all of this.

"Let me explain this to you Kamen. The guys in the white suit are under contract. They stay here for however many years then return to earth wealthy and rich, never having to work another day in their life," Maria explained.

"Never having to work again?" I asked.

"Kamen, my guys are practically doctors so they get paid a doctors salary. Now imagine working on a doctor's salary for years and not touching the money at all until your contract is up. That will make you one wealthy man," She said.

"I don't know, I have to think about it," I said.

"What is there to think about... are you missing anyone back on earth? You're mother sent you here is that correct?" Maria asked.

"Yea, she did," I replied.

"So I'm guessing she knows the importance of this place and won't care how long you're here as long as you graduate. I bet she would be very proud of you when she finds out you're a certified doctor," Maria said.

"I'll be a certified doctor? Does that mean I'll have to take some courses or something?" I asked.

"Nope, not at all. See my guys perform acts that only doctors can. There for I will have the pleasure of making you a certified doctor without you even trying," Maria explained. "You have only a couple minutes to decide Kamen, because I only have one more spot available. Now you are the first person I want to give it you but there are other potentials," Maria said.

Making this decision felt like the day I had to choice my classes. I knew I was smart enough to make this decision but the pressure of Mrs. Maria being there had me nervous. I tried to way in all my options as quickly as possible. "Alright, I'll do it. I'll work for you," I said. "Great, welcome to the team," Maria said. She hands me a cap and gown. "Now, here is your cap and gown because you can graduate with your class officially. But right after you gradate you are to change into your white suit and meet the rest of the team in the secret room in…." Maria began to say.

*The TV turns to a gray screen. "What, what happened?" Kamen asked. "I didn't press anything," Nikko replied.

*The TV turns back on.

"Kamen Johnson," The principal finally called my name. I walked up the stage to receive my certificate. This was the best day of my life. As I'm walking to receive my diploma I noticed group of men in white suits were waiting for me on stage. After I took my diploma they escorted me outside. They blind folded me. When I opened my eyes I was in some secret room that I've never seen before. There was a contract in front of me along with a sharp small knife and a pen.

** the TV screen turns gray and starts to static.

"Just wait for it," Nikko said.

*the tv turns back on.

"Welcome to team, Kamen Johnson," One the guys annouced.

*the tv shuts off completely.

I closed Kamen's folder. I then tried to open it again and it started from the very beginning.

"What, so that's it... I can't see what happens after that?" Kamen asked.

"Apparently not," I replied.

CHAPTER 11
ARE YOU IN OR OUT? CONTINUED

JOCELYN PULLS ME OFF to the side. "I don't know how much more I can take of this, please don't tell me I end up like that?" She asked.

"No, Jocelyn...you pass early and are successful but you don't need this school to be successful. You can go on planet earth and find another school," I said.

"On earth? There's no program like this on earth," Jocelyn replied.

"You can find one, and a better one at that," I replied.

"Why did you bring me here? If my future is just fine why are you trying to mess it up?" She questioned.

"Because, I thought you out of all people cared for justice for others," I replied.

"Justice, they could be studying like the rest of us," She said.

"But what about the people who haven't made their mind up or realize they got into the wrong profession?"

"Well that's their problem."

"What is with you Jocelyn?"

"What is with me? Are you forgetting how bad my mother struggles? Don't you wonder why I was always sleeping over at your house growing up? My mother works a dead end job nonstop to pay the bills and there is no one to watch me. Do you think I want that life? My mother is all that I have and we barley even see each other," Jocelyn said.

"My family has always welcomed you and treated you like family you know that. I'm sorry your mom has to work nonstop but that doesn't mean that will be your life…. And what about my sister huh, your best friend. She's coming to this school soon. Would you want to take the chance of her ending like anyone in that room? I asked.

"You're sister is smarter than that, she knows better," Jocelyn replied.

"Yea, I'm pretty sure everyone in that room said the same thing," I said.

"I got to go," Jocelyn said and stormed out the room.

I walk back in the room. "What happened, valedictorian decided she wasn't going to save the world today?" Nikko asked.

"She's just been tired… she's going to get some rest. For the rest of you, do I need to show you more?" I asked.

No one replied. "Okay, so now I only have one question. Are you in or out?"

"I'm in," Kelsey said, there's no way I'm going to risk not seeing my daughter again."

"Count me in," Mellissa replied.

"Me too," Carlos said. "Same here," Brianna said.

"I don't know what's worse. Not knowing what your future will be or staying in this school. And if those are my two options, I'm all in," Kamen said.

"I'm in too," Julia said.

We all waited for Lindsey's response.

"I don't know guys…" Lindsey said.

"It's up to you," I replied.

Nikko grabs a hold of Lindsey's file.

"Come on Nikko," I said.

"No, she doesn't know what she wants to do so let's give her a look at her future," Nikko replied.

Nikko opens Lindsey's file. Nikko holds down the fast forward button. Nikko pressed play and we watched as Lindsey eats out of trashcans to survive.

Lindsey starts gagging, "Okay, okay… I'm in," She said.

"Do you want to know how you got to this point?" Nikko asked.

"No, I don't… I said I'm in," Lindsey replied.

With studying for exams and trying to plan for mass destruction I became pretty restless. Trying to keep a high grade point average seemed impossible. Every morning the team and I practices fighting and got in a good work out. Mr. Jamison's class was my first class of the day, often the class I'm caught sleeping in. Mr. Jamison graded not only on the assignment but on punctuality. He watches your every move like a game of chess. He urged for you to advance in the class but didn't make it easy for you to do so.

My test scores came back from my psychology test. I passed with a C+. "Angel, may I speak with you?" Mrs. Jenkins asked. I knew this had to be about my performance in this class. "Angel, your test scores aren't looking so well," Mrs. Jenkins said.

"Yes, ma'am I know I'm trying my best," I replied.

"Well that's just not good enough. You are going to have to improve your average or I'm afraid you'll fail the class," She said.

My jaw dropped, "What do you mean I'm passing all of my assignments."

"Barley passing your assignments," She argued.

"Must I remind you this is preparation for 3rd floor training, if I don't think you're ready I will not pass you," Mrs. Jenkins said. I should have known this was coming.

After Psychology class I headed to the cafeteria. Jocelyn was obviously avoiding me. I grabbed some food then headed to the library to meet with everyone.

"There's something I want to talk to you guys about," I said then waited to get everyone's attention.

"I might not be making it to the 3rd floor."

Everyone starts fussing. "I knew this was all a joke," Lindsey said.

"What do you mean you're not going to make it? And Lindsey, that was a real image of your future so I surely wouldn't joke about that. Nikki said.

"Mrs. Jenkins is on my case about barley passing, she saying that I need to improve if I want to move on to the next level," I said.

"Ohh, easy fix...we'll study together," Nikki said.

"But I only have so much time," I replied.

"But you have enough time... don't worry, we're in this together," Nikki said.

We heard two females arguing in the library, they were getting pretty loud.

"Someone needs to stop them before they get in trouble," I suggested.

"Hey, I say let them cat fight...what's the worst that can happen?" Kamen replied.

"No, you have no idea..." I said. I started to get up to try to break up the fight but it was too late. The guys in white suits beat me to it. They broke up the fight and took the girls away.

I sighed, "There's one more thing I have to warn you guys about," I said.

"Okay, I am done with surprises," Julia said.

I didn't want to have this conversation in front of Nikki and Nikko, but I had no choice.

"If we are caught or fail in any way we too will be taken away by the gentleman in the white suits. Once taken away, we would be placed in this room where they would make us take these pills," I explained. Nikki couldn't take anymore of this conversation, she walks away.

"So, is that what my future would be if I were to become one of them?" Kamen asked.

"And what kind of pills exactly?" Brianna asked.

"I'm not one hundred percent sure what these pills do but I do know that you will be a changed person and under their control once you take it," I explained.

I took a deep breath, "If you resist taking these pills, they will kill you."

"What the fuck!" Brianna said.

"That's why it is very important for us to cover all of our bases and do everything accordingly," I replied.

"Yea, starting with you making it to the 3rd floor," Lindsey said.

I've had enough for today, see you guys tomorrow," She said.

Everyone else got up at once and left.

That night I studied for psychology class with Nikki.

"Nikki, today in the library...I'm sorry I had to bring that up," I said.

"It's okay, I need to be stronger for the people who would have come after me. I know my parents would be proud of me," She said.

"How's your sister holding up?" I asked.

"Oh she's a strong girl, she'll be fine. She just wants a better life for the both of us. She is the oldest you know…by two seconds," Nikki said.

We looked over and Nikko tossing in her sleep, knocking the blanket off of body. Nikki walks over and fixes the blanket for her sister.

Nikki heads to bed, "Goodnight Angel."

"Goodnight Nikki."

The next morning everyone was ready for a good workout. Instead of our regular workout routine I wanted to step it up a notch. "Everyone pick you're partners," I announced. "Once you pick your partner, turn around and face them," I said. I waited for everyone to get in position. "Uh, I don't have a partner," Lindsey said. I stood in front of Lindsey, "Now you do."

"I want everyone to take a couple steps back," I said while taking 3 steps back. Now, get ready to fight," I said.

"Fight? But…." Brianna said.

"But what?" I replied.

I waited for everyone to get in fighting stance.

I stomped my foot on the ground and snarled at Lindsey.

"Let's go!" I took charge at Lindsey.

My days here became pretty repetitive. I worked out, went to class, got food, worked out again, than studied with Nikki. The rest of the team was getting better each day in martial arts. Sadly, there was still no show from Jocelyn. My test grades were improving in psychology. My grades went from a C – to a B+ but I still wasn't sure if that was good enough for Mrs. Jenkins.

The team and I sat together during lunch. We discussed the plan before our food arrived. Then when it did, we just sat together and enjoyed our lunch. I got out my seat to get some napkins. I ran into Thomas on the way. "So those are you're new friends huh?" he stopped me. "What happened to Iris, Valerie, or even Jocelyn?" he asked. "You don't understand," I replied. "Maybe so because you don't speak to me," he replied. I walked away to get some napkins, he follows behind me. "Maybe I don't speak to you because you simply just couldn't comprehend if you tried. Like I said, you don't understand," I said. I brushed past him.

A group of gentleman in white suits walked in the cafeteria. Each of them had folders in their hand. They stood around the middle table. Maria walks in and makes her way to the middle table. When she arrives, they all take their seats. "I wonder what's going on," Brianna asked. "Yea, me too," Nikki said. "I'm sure we'll find out sooner or later," Nikko replied. We watched as they stood up. Maria hands the gentleman the folders and they exit the cafeteria. Maria stands in the center of the cafeteria and said, "Students may I have your attention."

She waits for everyone to silence.

"Thank you all, I am pleased to announce the list is up for our graduates moving forward to the 3rd floor," Maria announced.

Everyone rushed into the halls. "I'm nervous," I whimpered.

"Don't be… with all that studying we did," Nikki replied. Nikki and I walked over to the hallway. "You look for me, I can't," I said. Nikki looks through the list to find my name. Her voice softens, "Well, Angel…." She takes a long pause then screamed, "You made it!" I jumped with joy and relieve. The rest of the team gathers behind me. "I made it you guys!" They all cheered.

That night the school threw us party to celebrate. "It's about time we have some fun around here," Julia said. Everyone was dancing and having a good time. I wanted to find my old friends to see what they were having a good time. I noticed Valerie and Iris dancing together. I decided to join them. "I miss you guys," I said.

"You miss us? But we've been here the whole time," Valerie said. "No, I miss the old Valerie and Iris…you know before we came to this school," I continued. They started laughing and continued dancing. I grabbed them by the arm, "You guys don't remember how close we used to be? You guys don't miss our friend ship?" I asked. They gave me a confusing look as if they didn't know what I was talking about. "Come on you guys we had sleepovers all the time at my house. Do you guys remember when we joined the volleyball team together and went to the championship? Then our parents took us all to the beach to celebrate? I asked. They looked at me with bank faces. I wanted to say more but I didn't bother wasting my breath.

I met up with the team by the snack table. "Even the snack table only has vegetable sticks, go figure," Brianna said.

"You guys want to get out of here?" I asked.

"Well it's about time someone said it," Nikko replied.

Thomas walks towards me as we are headed out the door. He stands there with Mike and Ryan. "Hey, you're not going to stay and enjoy the party?" he asked. "No sorry, I have to run," I replied.

We trained in our dresses because we didn't bring our workout gear. This time I fought against Nikko and it was definitely my most challenging fight. I looked at the window and noticed Thomas watching us. He must have followed me. Nikko rips a hole in my dress and pins me to the ground. "Don't get caught being distracted. You're real friends would have been there for you no matter what," She said. I got up and started fighting back. Nikko hit me causing me to run into the door. "You need to forget about them for now, they will only hold you back," Nikko said as she pins to the floor once more. I watched as Thomas left. I stayed there on the floor, thinking of what Nikko said.

CHAPTER 12
GRADUATION DAY

Nikko, Nikki and I were all packed and ready for the third floor. It felt like it took forever to get to this point. We got on the elevator. Nikko and I watched as Nikki dramatically pressed the number 3. "This is it… the last floor," Nikki said. A holographic image appeared in the elevator. "Please choice your size" We read on screen. The screen had an image of an outfit for woman and men that resembled a space suit but more fitting. After we each picked out size's the elevator suddenly stopped. A secret department opened inside the elevator with a note, "Please Take" on it. "Woah, no way… this look's even better than the picture," I said as we looked at our new uniforms. The uniforms were black and white with "AI" labeled on the front pocket.

"Okay, so why isn't the elevator moving?" Nikko asked. "Maybe we have to press the button again?" Nikki said. We then heard from the intercom, "You must put uniforms on before entering the 3rd floor". "So we have to change right here?" Nikki asked. Nikko starts taking off her shirt, "I guess so," she said. We changed our clothes. "Okay, we're done" I announced. The elevator finally goes up to the 3rd floor.

We walked on the 3rd floor. The walls were titanium with blue lights. There weren't nearly as much people as the previous floors. We walked the halls, looking for our dorm room. Thomas spots me in the hall, "Glad to see you made it, Angel," He said.

"Likewise Thomas," I continued walking.

"Marley didn't make it Angel, neither did Ryan," He said.

My heart dropped, "They didn't make it...but didn't they all attend of the celebration party?" I asked.

"Yea, but I guess things didn't go as planned," Thomas replied.

"Did they say anything to you?" I asked.

"No, that's the strangest part about it...they were perfectly fine with staying behind.

Ryan even said, "Only for the better," So he could practice more to get better.

I glanced over at Nikki and Nikko waiting for me.

"Why don't you just think about that Thomas, I have to go," I replied.

"No Christy and Kelly tour on this floor I see," I said.

"Good, I got tired of hearing their perky voices over and over again, Nikko replied.

"Yea, they are like the cheerleaders of this school huh?" I suggested.

We found our room; it is the same layout as the 2nd floor.

Nikko throws herself on her bed, "Ahhh, new floor...same bed."

"New floor, same you?" I asked.

"Nope...I'd like to say this suit makes me feel stronger and better," she replied.

"You guys hungry?" I asked.

"Are we...." Nikki replied. We headed to the cafeteria.

The cafeteria was way fancier than the other floors. Beautiful chandeliers hung from the ceiling. The room was filled long white tables and blue chairs. We stood in line at the salad bar and made our plates. "I can't believe they didn't make it," I said. "Who?" Nikki replied.

"Marley and Ryan, they didn't make it here. And from that Thomas said, they are perfectly fine with that," I replied.

"Why are you surprised? Didn't they take the pill?" Nikko asked.

The team walks over to the table. Nikki, Nikko and I Cheer.

We laugh as everyone in the cafeteria stares at us.

I whispered, "Gangs all here, now let's shake things up."

We start the day with workout. I watched everyone and they seemed to be slacking and becoming lazy. I stood in the middle of the room.

"I can't, I just can't watch this. You guys need to step it up and tap in to your highest potential. It's time to use the strength deep inside of you that you may not even know you have. Remember, we are not just doing this for us and our future… But, we are doing this for the next generation's future. So that no one is stuck working a job they dislike because of one decision made at this school. No one is restricted from spending quality time with their family. And so no one has to spend the rest of their life living like a slave, working for them. I need more, from all you," I preached.

I watched them as they fought harder than they ever had. Nikko walks over to me, "The boss said she wants more… let's give her more," she said. She gets into stance to fight and looks me in the eyes. I took a couple steps towards her and took my stance. She takes charge at me and starts fighting. I block every swing she threw at me. I spun around and kicked her, causing her to fall to the ground. "If you thought this was going to be like our other fights you got another thing coming," I said. Nikko trips me and tries to pin me to the ground. I jump up and start fighting back. I suddenly stop, "You guys hear that?"

Nikko tries to take advance and pins me down. I get up and pin her down, "Seriously Nikko," I said. "Everybody, stop what you're doing and sit down!" I yelled. I quickly got up. Everyone looked confused as they sat down on the floor. I ran to my book bag and grabbed the first school book I could find. I ran back to everyone and pretended to read to them. "What is she doing?" Julia whispered to Nikko.

"I have no idea," Nikko replied. That very moment Maria walks past. Maria walks in the room. "Oh what honorable students you all are to be studying this early," Maria said. "Keep up the good work," She said then left the room. "Woo, that was a close one… how did you know she was coming?" Kamen asked. "You can hear those heels from a mile away," I replied. We continued our training afterwards. We fought until we couldn't fight anymore.

My body was sore by the time we finished. I took a quick shower then got ready for Mr. Jamison's class. Today was presentation day for our project. I must admit, it felt good to stick with the same teacher on each level. I walked in the class room and each student had a sample of their projects in their hands. Mr. Jamison walks in the room. "Please, students... gather your projects and follow me," He said. He took us to a conference room with one large round table and a large screen. "Students, please take your seats," Mr. Jamison said. He stands in front of the room and waits for us to all take our seats. "Who wants to go first?" he asked. "I'll go," a class mate was eager to present his project. He displayed his miniature car in his hand then started his presentation.

The rest of my classes went by like a breeze. The only class I was worried about was Psychology, my last class of the day. I walked to class but was stopped on the way there. It was the Television industry teacher from the first floor. "Angel right?" he asked. "I wanted to speak to you before you graduate," he said. I had no idea was this conversation was going to be about. "I watched the short video you made in class," he said. I was embarrassed, "that was recording the whole time?" I asked. He started laughing. "It was perfect, I really thought you were going to join my class," he said. I put my head down and replied, "Yea... I wanted to but..."

"But what, you were afraid of everything I told you not to be afraid of?" he asked.

"Yea, I guess," I replied.

"So what course did you end up taking?" he asked.

"Psychology," I said.

He gave me a look on uncertainty.

"Well, too bad it's too late to switch... you would have made a wonderful host, or anything TV personality for that matter. You have power in your voice, I can feel it" he said.

"Thank you, everything happens for a reason right. Maybe one day I will be," I replied.

"Sorry kid, but not in this universe, it's already too late," he replied.

I was late to class by a couple of seconds. The door was already shut and the teacher looked like she didn't want to let me in. She opens the door, "I'm being very generous letting you join my class room after the bell rang, next time I won't be so nice," She said. "Sorry about that, won't happen again," I replied. I quickly walked inside and took a seat next to Nikki.

"Alright class let's get straight to it. My name is Mrs. Lola and I will be your teacher," She said. "Lola like Lola bunny?" My class mate asked. Mrs. Lola started taping her pen on her desk. "What is your name sir?" Mrs. Lola asked.

"Brandon," he replied.

Mrs. Lola makes a phone call on her phone.

Mrs. Lola begins passing out our new Psychology books. "Students, please begin readying Chapter 4," She said.

Minutes later the guys in white suits entered the class.

"You have got to be kidding me," I whispered to Nikki.

The guys in white suits walked towards Brandon and escorted him out the classroom.

"Students, let that be an example for you. I will not tolerate foolishness in this classroom. You're former classmate Brandon, will be returning to the 1st floor because of his actions," She said.

"She's no joke," Nikki whispered.

I was very relieved when the I heard the bell ring; being in Mrs. Lola's class made me feel like a hostage in jail. I walked the halls, trying to learn the ends and outs. I had everything in order and perfectly constructed for mass destruction. Only thing I was missing was the location of the vortex. "What are you doing here, shouldn't you be eating dinner?" Maria asked as she stopped me in the halls. "Oh, I just wanted to give myself a tour of the 3rd floor. It feels weird without Christy and Kelly," I said. "Oh...Well come, I will give you a tour myself," Maria replied.

Maria walked me through the halls. "What about the counselor's office where is that located?" I asked. She walked me to the counselor's office. I was hoping the secret vortex would be there. "What about if I ever need to speak to you... about anything, where could I find you?" I asked. "My office, come this way..." She said. We walked in front of a wall, I questioned why. "Here, you would press this button and ask for me," Maria said. "Because behind these walls is where my office is located," She said. She entered in a code on the wall. Five, seven, six, one, three, two, seven, three, five, one, were the list of numbers. I repeated those numbers over and over in my head.

The secret door opened and we headed inside. There were two gentlemen in white suits standing there as is they were guarding her office. I knew the vortex had to be located in here somewhere. "This is my office where you are only aloud to come if you really need me," She explained. "Now, I actually have some work to do and you should get going to dinner," She said. "Thank you for the tour," I said. I quickly ran to the nearest classroom. I wrote the pass code down on a piece of paper before I could forget.

Each day in Mathematics class another student presented their projects. My classmates invested in things like: Computers, trade stocks, parking lots, furniture stores, and starting their own business. Psychology class was stiff and boring. I was always afraid of getting in trouble in her class for any little thing. Mrs. Lola always reminded us that we could be placed back on the 1st floor.

The last day of class and everyone had already presented their projects to the class. Mr. Jamison announced the winner to be my class mate, Stephanie. Stephanie started with one investment then predicted to double the amount with investment stocks and trades. "The key to investing students is taking risk that you are confident in," Mr. Jamison said. "Stephanie here invested in several different investments and planned accordingly each year how she would use them to not only makes her a lot of money but help the economy. "Stephanie, please explain to the class what you plan to do after you graduate," Mr. Jamison said. "I plan to become a telemarketer to advance my knowledge and continue investing in trademarks until I am able to quit my job and start my own business. Her numbers project 500 Billion by the age of 40," Mr. Jamison explains. I guess I should have taken a closer look at her folder. The class clapped from Stephanie. My classmates started passing up their fake money. "Sucks, this fake money actually made me believe I was going to be rich one day," I said. "Oh, you are more than welcome to keep your money Angel. It may help you one day as a motivation," Mr. Jamison said.

In psychology, Mrs. Lola constantly reminded us that anything in the world could easily be taken from us. I walked in the classroom and the set up was completely different. "Students, it's time to live your life here as your future will be on earth," Mrs. Lola said. The classroom desks were now office desk. Each desk had a laminated copy of each of our names. Besides each of our desk was reclining chairs. It was the perfect set up for therapy sessions. I took my seat at my desk. Folders were stacked on top of the desk with client names on each. I closed my eyes and kept visioning the counselor's office. I was seeing my classmate's future over and over again in my head. "Today's class assignment you will prepare therapy sessions for each of your clients," Mrs. Lola said.

The day we've all been waiting for has finally arrived. It was Graduation day! The morning of was nerve wrecking and anticipating. I put on my suit under my graduation gown. I gathered up with the team early in the morning and went over the plan once more with them. I was glad that everyone was on board and ready. Everyone passed their courses with straight A's and even Kamen showed more enthusiasm to pass the course. Each of them seemed ready and eager. "Students, please report to the auditorium for graduation," We heard over the intercom. "It's time," I said.

Everyone took their places for mass destruction. Maria took the stage as the graduating students took their seats. I was not with the rest of them; I was on the way to Maria's office. The first step I had to complete was getting inside; the second was getting past the two guys guarding the door. I put Maria's pass code in. My first attempted worked and the doors began opening. I could hear the graduation speech going on, on the TV's in her office.

"Hey, what are you doing back here?" The guy guarding the door asked. I quickly jumped up and power kicked him. The other guy grabs me from behind. I run backwards and bang my head against his, causing his to hit the wall. The other guy gets up from the ground and charges at me, I kicked him once more. The two guys were face first on the floor. I ran around the office, looking for the vortex but it was nowhere in sight.

I suddenly heard the sound of sirens through the loud speaker. I ran to the front and one of the guards was missing. Before I knew it, the guard was grabbing my arms from behind. I struggled to get out. I tried to kick my feet back. "Not this time, little girl," He said. The alarm sounded, which means Kamen should have turned off the elevators, forcing no one to enter the third neither floor nor exit. The guard escorts me through the halls. When Maria was told someone tried to break into her office, she quickly ran from her podium. Lindsey as Kelsey job was to lock everyone in the auditorium. Maria calls for defensive team.

Julia was the lookout for me in the hall. As soon as the guard and I reach the hallway she hits the guard above the head, causing him to fall to the ground. "What happened?" Julia asked. "The vortex wasn't there," I replied. "So what's the plan?" Julia asked as we heard banging sounds coming from the auditorium. "After a student graduates and receives their certificate, where are they told to go?" I asked. "They are told to follow the direction behind the curtains," Julia said. I slapped my hand, "The vortex must be behind the curtains," I said. "Let's go!"

Keman runs towards our direction. "I tried to hold off the elevators as fast as I could but they are overriding me," He said. We hear the footsteps of men heading our direction. "You guy ready?" I asked. "Ready!" They replied.

It was time to battle the men in white suits. When they spotted us, they took charge. One guy ran over to open the doors of the auditorium, Keman followed behind him. Julia and I used our fighting skills to nearly knock out most of the men but there were too many of them. I guess Keman couldn't stop the gentleman from opening the doors because we heard the loud rupture of student's voices. We ran inside to find the rest of the team in the midst of the kayos.

We met up with everyone but Brianna and Carlos, they were nowhere to be found. Students were running around panicking. Guards were on stage with Maria. "There's no way we can reach the vortex this way," Nikki said. "Let's go around to the back," I ordered. Each of us spread out. Suddenly a hand full of students all stopped moving at once. The other students followed their lead. They all turned and looked towards Maria as if they were under some sort of brain stimulus.

Maria took her stance once more on the podium. "Students, we have a disruption on at this school. We need your help to stop this disruption and capture the disobedient students. Did I make myself clear?" Maria asked. "Yes, Mrs. Maria," the students replied. I stood in the midst of them to blend in. "Find these students to help return this school back to order!" She ordered. "Yes, Mrs. Maria," The students replied.

I walked quickly towards the door while trying to blend in with the rest of the students. I ran into Thomas and Jocelyn. Jocelyn stops me before I could reach the door. "Do you have something to do with this?" She asked. I tried to keep walking and Thomas stands in front of the door. "Angel what's going on?" he asked. I whispered as the students eased dropped on our conversation, "I had no other choice." "So it was you?" Jocelyn repeated in anger. "So what if it was, not everyone is going to have a set future like you Jocelyn," I replied. "What do you plan on doing Angel?" Thomas asked. "Why would I tell you Thomas, you never believed me and you still won't," I replied. I headed to the doors.

As soon as I put my hands on the door handle I hear Jocelyn scream, "Here she is!" Every student in the 3rd level who was giving the pill turns at me. With their glaring eyes they start charging at me. I start fighting the students, but there was too many of them. Nikko and Nikki make their way to the crowd and help me break free from the students. We stood in the middle of the students, ready to fight for our freedom. "Angel you don't have to do this!" Jocelyn screamed. "It's ether fight for the life I want or struggle to survive the life I don't!" I yelled. I took charge at the door and fought the students blocking the exit.

Marley was outside of the door when I finally was able to break free. She was standing there by herself in the corner. Nikki and Nikko come behind me and block the door from opening. "Marley, what's going on?" I asked. "Ever since I saw my future…I've been afraid to actually fight," She said. "You're future is whatever you make it as of now Marley," I replied. Nikki and Nikko struggle to hold the doors closed. "You can't be afraid your whole life, you are stronger than before Marley… I believe in you," I said. "We can't hold this door any longer!" Nikki yelled.

The doors open and the students burst through the halls. Nikki starts fighting with the students while Nikko and I run to find the vortex. As Nikki struggles to fight the students alone, the guys in white suits run towards Marley. Marley runs away. I head in the opposite direction with Nikko. Nikko didn't want to leave her sister behind. "We don't have much time, we have to end this," I said. "You're right…and it ends now," Maria said. She stands there with about four men in white suits. "Get them," She commanded. That moment Thomas comes out of the corner and sprays

Maria and the guys in the white suits with the fire extinguisher. Nikko and I run away, Thomas follows.

We take a detour to get to the back of the auditorium. "Those students, fighting you guys...are those the ones who have been given the pill?" Thomas asked. "Now do you believe me?" I questioned. We turned the corner and Maria was on the other end standing there. She knew exactly what we were after. "Silly silly students... I've been trained black belt for almost 200 hundred years now," Maria said as she takes off her white coat and reveals her suit under. I rush at her and she blocks my hits and pushes me against the wall. "Is that all you got?" She asked as she gets into fighting stance. "You guys go, I want this fight," Nikko said.

Thomas and I run the other direction. We are stopped by three men in white suits. Julia and Kamen rush over to us. "We got this, go.." Kamen said. Thomas and I continued running. We made it to the back of the auditorium. I heard the loud swirling sounds behind the second curtains. "It must be back there," I said. As Thomas drops the curtains, I noticed Valerie standing there guarding the vortex.

"Valerie, listen... you don't know what you're doing," I said as I walk towards her. Valerie shoves me down and pushes me to the ground. "Okay, now I definitely believe you," Thomas said as he helps me back up. Two men in white suits come towards us. "I'll take care of them," Thomas said. Thomas didn't know how to fight. He's lanky arms and legs did the job the best way he could to hold them off. Nikki arrives and helps him fight the guys while I attempted to get past Valerie.

"Valerie, it's me.. you're friend.. we grew up together Valerie," I said. Valerie stands there with a blank face ready to attack. "Okay, I'm just going to..." I begin to try to get past her but she pushes me down once again. I looked in the corner of my eyes and the team was heading towards my way. The guys in white suits were chasing behind them. I got up and charged at Valerie. "I love you Val, but I can't let you stop me," I said. I fought her and she was giving me a good run for my money. She pushed me against the wall, causing a glass mirror to break. I knocked her down with everything I had. I ran to the vortex.

"Plug in the reverse code!" Keman screamed. I opened my bag to find the reserve code then quickly started plugging in the numbers. I was almost finished then I heard Nikki scream, "Watch out!" Valerie had a glass piece in her hand as she charges to me. I move out the way and Valerie runs into the wall. The glass piece cuts her stomach. Valerie was bleeding all over the place. I screamed, "Valerie!" when I saw her loosing so much blood. I burst into tears. My hands were shaking I could barley finish the code. I heard, "Valerie, Valerie," from Jocelyn running towards her crying. I wanted to throw up. Nikko runs up the stairs limping. "Finish it!" She screams. I rushed as fast as I could to finish the reverse code. Jocelyn run towards me, "No, don't do it!" I hit enter and the Vortex explodes.

CHAPTER 13
I DIDN'T WANT THIS

I WOKE UP TO my sister was blasting her music. I was back in my bed at home on planet Earth. I got up and ran to my sister, who was doing her makeup. "Yvette... how long have I been here?" I asked. "What kind of question is that.. umm, pretty much all your life," She replied. "I meant since I've been away, how long has it been since I've been back?" I asked. Yvette looks at me confused, "What do you mean...where did you go?" She asked. "You mean I never left to *Atlas Institution*?" I asked. "What are you talking about?" Yvette asked as she continues to put on her makeup.

I sat back on my bed to gather my thoughts. When Yvette was finally finished with her makeup she comes over to see what's going on with me. "Are you wearing contacts?" She asked. My heart dropped, I ran to the bathroom. My eyes have changed colors to a light blue. Yvette starts knocking on the door. "Why aren't you getting ready for school and since when did mom let you wear contacts?" She asked.

I opened the door. "School?" I asked. "Yes, High School... a place where you learn. How long are you going to keep this act going on?" She asked. "It just ended," I replied as I rushed to put on my clothes for school. I quickly got dressed and headed to school with my sister.

We stopped at the store to get contacts for me before heading to school. Once we arrived to school, we parked in the student parking lot and walked to the building. I've never seen the inside of a high school before but this is how I imagined it. I noticed School mascots, cheerleaders, punks, musicians, jocks, and everything else in between.

My sister meets up with her friends. I was still trying to fathom what was going on. I walked in the cafeteria. The students were having breakfast. I spotted Thomas with his friend Ryan. "Thomas! Oh my gosh," I ran to him and gave him a big hug. He didn't show too much enthusiasm to see me. "Hey, Angel...What's going on?"

"I have so much to talk to you about Thomas, can you believe we made it back?"

"Made it back?"

"Yea... to..." I began to say. I looked around to his group of friends and I didn't feel very welcomed.

I whispered to Thomas, "What's going on, why are they looking at me like that?"

"Like what? And Angel we haven't hung out since we were little. What do you have to talk to me about?"

"Oh... well, never mind then. I'll see you around,"

I got up from my seat. "Why were you talking to that black girl?" I heard his friend say as I walked away. I didn't even bother turning around.

"Black girl? Is that what people know each other as on earth, by their skin color?" I asked myself.

I left the cafeteria. I needed to find someone that remembered *Atlas Institution*. I was slowly losing my sanity. I searched around the school like a hound dog looking for anyone that was at *Atlas Institution* with me. I suddenly spotted Nikki and Nikko. They were sitting on the floor in the hallway readying their books. "Nikki, Nikko!" I yelled. As they put their book down I could tell they didn't remember from their look of confusion. I didn't bother explaining anything to them, I just continued walking.

I sat down in the hallway. I started recognizing familiar faces. My team was here, Carlos, Brianna, Julia, Kamen, Lindsey, and Kelsey. They were all chatting with their friends. The bell rings. I didn't know what my first class but I was sure to find out by going through my book bag. I started searching through my bag then felt a tap on my shoulder. "Hey girl, why aren't you heading to class?" Valerie asked. I jumped up and hugged her for dear life. "Oh my gosh, Valerie...I can't believe I'm looking at you right now," I stopped hugging her and took a long look at her. "Valerie, my friend..." My eyes started to water.

"What's wrong, you're acting like you're never going to see me again? You miss school for one day and the world is upside down," She said. "You have no idea. I am just happy to see you thats all," I replied. "Okay well let's go before we're late to class," She said. "Val, I haven't been myself lately so I'm going to need you to catch me up on a lot of things," I said. "Sure, no problem," She said as we walked the halls to class. "First thing, what class are we going to?" I asked. "Math class...then you are going to science and I'm going to gym class," She replied.

"Hey, there's your sister and Jocelyn," Valerie said as they walked the opposite side of the halls. I wasn't too thrilled to see my sister associating herself with Jocelyn. I continued walking as if I didn't see them while Valerie stopped to say hello. Valerie runs to catch up to me. "That was weird, why didn't you stop?" Valerie asked. "Oh, I'll see my sister at home," I replied. "And Jocelyn?" she asked. "Yea... I don't know about her," I said. "What do you mean she's over at your house all the time, I mean that is you're sister's best friend," Valerie explained. "Yea..I wouldn't say best friend..that's a strong word," I replied.

Before I passed the classroom Valerie stopped me. We walked in and took our assigned seats. I was assigned to the seat next to Thomas and it never felt more uncomfortable. The teacher walks in the class. "Students, please take out your geometry homework and start the assignment on the board," She said. I looked up at the board and had no clue how to solve the assignment. I knew this was going to be a long day.

I was so relieved to hear the bell ring. I watched as Valerie rushed out the classroom. I followed behind her. "Wait!" I yelled.

"Don't tell me you don't know where your classes are at ether?" She asked.

Valerie takes me to my science class then writes down the list of my classes down for me in order with directions to how to get to each one. I walked into my science class that was more like a science lab. The students were putting on their lab coats and gloves. I followed their lead. "What's that smell?" I asked my classmate. "Oh that smell is our project. Did you forget? We are dissecting frogs today," My corky classmate eagerly explained.

We all got into groups of four. The teacher brings over dead frogs to each group to insect. Splat! I looked over and a frog has hit the floor. "Now, Mike...you are in the eleventh grade now. It's time to grow up," The science teacher said. Mike walks over to pick the frog up. He puts the frog in front of his face. "Who wants to kiss the frog to save their life?" He asked. The class laughs. This wasn't the Mike I knew. The Mike I knew was funny but he never played around in class.

After science class was over it was time to lunch. I ran to the concession stand and brought sprinkled donuts. I've never been so happy to see donuts in my life. I then went in the lunch line and got a fat juicy burger. I sat down and started grubbing down on my delicious burger. I looked up and everyone was staring at me. "I haven't eaten all morning," I replied. I noticed as Marley walks holding hands with some guy. They sat down and started making out in the cafeteria. "No PDA students," a teacher said to Marley. As soon as the teacher left, Marley and her boyfriend continued kissing.

My last class of the day was Gym class. I walked in the gym and everyone was sitting in a circle. The gym teacher walks over with her whistle around her neck and clip board in her hand. "Okay class, today we are having free day so I can get things done so... you're welcome," She said. My class mates all dispersed after our teacher walked away. The gym was filled with multiple different classes and everyone was having a free day to enjoy any activity. Students were playing basketball, volleyball, ping pong and other activities.

I walked over to the dart board and picked up some darts. I start throwing the darts but was missing everyone. My gym teacher drops her clip board and walks over to me as if I was in trouble. "Angel, you're doing this all wrong," She said as she grabs one the darts. "You have to focus and aim," She said as she gets in stance and waves the darts back and forth. She releases the dart and hits target, I was impressed.

I tried to concentrate but I had so much on my mind. I had so many thoughts running through my head. I cleared my mind and aimed the dart. I kept attempting to hit the target. I then put all my energy and focus in hitting the target. I pulled my hand back and focused on the target. I threw the dart and hit the target. I felt a magnetic force. My body shook. I turned around and everyone in the gym was moving in slow motion. I didn't fight this feeling, I tried to channel it. As I'm focusing a classmate walks in front of me. I slowly bumped into the classmate. I looked him in the eyes and something magical happen. I was able to see into his future.

I tried to make my way to the other end of the gym but I was also moving in slow motion. Whenever I got really close to someone and focused on them I was able to see their future. I was losing my mind at this moment. I walked as fast as I possibly could to the locker room. When I left the gym I took a couple deep breaths and tried to relax my body. I took another look in the gym and everything was back to normal. I then ran to the locker room and shut the door. I looked at myself in the mirror. I focused on myself and tried to remember everything I could about graduation day. I was able to get in tune with myself and remember the Vortex exploding. That was the moment my eyes changed colors because of the radioactive waves. I was given power from the vortex to seek into the future.

That night I sat at the dinner table with my family. My mom cooked some meatloaf, mash potatoes, and cornbread. My mother's cooking taste like heaven in my mouth. "Uh, Angel.. did you not eat lunch today?" my dad asked as he watched me stuff my face. "I did, but I just missed mom's cooking so much," I replied. "See, it's about time someone appreciates my cooking around here," She argues. The door bell rings, it was Jocelyn. "Jocelyn, we are glad to have you for dinner...take a seat," My mother said. My sister and Jocelyn start having their own conversation.

"So girls, how was school?" my mother asked. "Ehh, school was school," Yvette said. "And you, Jocelyn?" My mother asked. "I enjoyed school, learned a lot today about autonomy," Jocelyn replied. "See, you girls need to be more like Jocelyn," My mother said. I started chocking on my food after hearing that. "Drink some water Angel," My dad said. "I'm all done, I need to work on my homework anyway," I said. I put my dish away and quickly left the kitchen.

I went to my room and opened my binder. I start flipping through the pages of my previous class assignments. I had to realize that this was my life now so I began studying for my classes. I studied for Math, English, Science, and History class. It was now 1am and I was exhausted. "Where is my major course? What am I studying to be?" I asked myself as I'm flipping through all of my notebooks. I couldn't stay awake any longer and I fell asleep.

The next day of school I tried to act like a regular student. I went throughout my classes and completed my assignments like everyone else. I even tried to connect with my old team in attempt to become their friend. During lunch I walked over to Julia and took a seat next to her. "Hey, what's up?"

"Nothing much... just eating lunch,"

"My name is Angel, What's yours?"

"Julia."

"Well nice to meet you Julia, I believe you're class is in gym last period with mine?"

"Oh yea.. I am, now I remember you. I don't like talking to strangers you know there's some weirdo's at this school."

"I bet, so what class do you have before gym?"

"Math, but I fucking hate it...I think I'm just going to leave with a group of friends and smoke a blunt after lunch. Then my last class is Gym and we barley to anything in there."

"But what about Math class, aren't you going to need to learn that. What are you trying to do in the future?"

"Yea, about that.. I'm not sure yet, I still haven't decided."

"That's okay... but what are you thinking about doing?"

"What are you, my mom?" Julia asked as her friend's flag her down. "You down to come smoke then head to gym together?" She asked.

"No I'm okay, I'll see you in gym class," I replied.

I watched Julia leave the cafeteria with her group of friends. I wanted to see her future before she left so I tried to focus. By the time I was focused, Julia had already left the cafeteria but the cafeteria was now in slow motion. I looked over at Marley and focused on her instead. Her boyfriend was walking towards her. She had the biggest smile on her face. Her future was glare as her boyfriend interfered with my thought process. The image suddenly became clear. Marley was going to get pregnant and drop out of school. Marley and her boyfriend end up splitting up after not having enough money to pay the bills. Marley is stuck raising the baby on her own. My heart saddened for Marley as I watched her struggle.

I then noticed students slowly making their way outside. I relaxed my body to come back to reality. I ran outside to see what all the commotion was about. I watched as the police officers are arresting some students. I walked towards the front of the crowd. It was Julia, getting busted for smoking on school property.

The principal orders the students to get back inside the building. Yvette and Jocelyn were standing inside. "What happened?" Yvette asked. "Couple students got caught smoking outside," I replied. "Who?" she asked. "Oh I don't know any of them but one, Julia," I replied. "Oh that girl, she hasn't learned her lesson yet?" Yvette said. Yvette and Jocelyn start laughing. "That girl is going to end up a damn druggy if she keeps this up," Yvette said. "Oh I can definitely see that," Jocelyn replied.

"Yvette what do you plan on doing after high school?" I asked. "I'm going to become a nurse... you know this," She replied. "But you hate the sign of blood, how are you going to handle that?" I replied. "I don't know...I'll figure it out and my best friend will help me," Yvette said. "You're studying to become a doctor right?" I asked Jocelyn. "Yea, I want to but let's face it, there's no way I'm going to be able to afford school," she said.

Gym was my favorite class because it was a chance for me to let off some steam. Today, we were outside playing a fun game of softball. I was in center field. My class mate hits the ball and it comes straight towards me. The ball goes over my head and I start running for it. Then out of nowhere another ball comes towards me, causing me to miss the other ball. "Hold on, hold on. Go ahead and pass that other ball back to the boys," My gym teacher said. I grabbed the other ball and ran to the fence. Carlos was the one who hit the ball over the fence. I threw it over to his coach. "Alright, that's what I'm talking about. Future major league player right there!" his coach yelled. I ran back over to the softball team and continued the game.

After the game was over we all headed to the locker room. My body was sweaty and my head was spinning from being in the heat all day. I chugged some water down. My head was still spinning. Everyone's voices grew louder and louder to the point where I couldn't hear myself think. As I looked at everyone their future started appearing in thin air. It was too much for me to bear at this point. I changed as fast as I could but I kept feeling like someone was screaming at me. I held my ears together and buried myself in my locker. I sat there trembling until everyone was gone.

I woke up the next morning and wasn't looking forward to another day at school. A stayed in bed while my sister blast her music while getting ready. "Hello, we're going to be late!" Yvette yelled. I pulled the covers from over my head. "I'm not feeling to good Yvette, tell mom please," I said. My mom overheard us, "Tell mom what?" She asked. Yvette left the room. "I'm not feeling good, I can't make it out of bed," I told her. "What do you mean you can't make it out of bed, you were just fine yesterday," She replied. "Mom I really can't, I feel like I'm about to…" I ran to the bathroom and pretended to throw up. "Alright you can stay home today but you better take some medicine and I'm emailing all of your teachers to get your homework" She said.

I waited for everyone to leave the house. As soon as I heard my mother's car take off I jumped out of bed. "Woo," I said out of relieve. I went in the kitchen to make me some breakfast and watched TV. I flipped the channels and found world's best investors. I smiled as I thought about Mr. Jamison's class. A part of me was missing *Atlas Institution*. The other part of me was just happy to be able to eat whatever I want.

I destroyed *Atlas Institution* to give each student a better fate for their future. What I didn't know is that they were only going to be less interested in creating a good future for themselves. I had to undo what I did or fix this somehow. I grabbed construction paper and my year book. I glued my friend's faces to the construction paper. I then drew arrows with the words, before and after above them. I wrote down the future of each person before and after *Atlas Institution* was destroyed.

I sat there and thought of possible things to do. I focused my mind to come up with any conclusion. I looked up and saw a stack of folders on my desk. I started thinking about the room in the counselor's office. I looked over at the folders then looked at each person's face. Something about Psychology kept popping in my head and I tried to figure out why. I held the folder tight in my hand and envisioned myself at my desk in

Psychology class. That's when I thought of the idea to become a therapist here on earth, so this way I could figure out what is going through my friends head and others.

I had to think of a way to become a therapist; I mean I was already technically qualified. I thought of all possibilities and everything that could go wrong. I gathered up all my information I knew about my friends and created a file for each of them.

The next day I had to seem like I was getting over a cold so my mom wouldn't think I lied about being sick. I had tissue in my hand and sniffled in the morning while getting ready. "How are you feeling Angel?" My mother asked. "I'm feeling a little better mom, thank you," I replied. As soon as I walked in the school building I ran to the restroom. I put one of my mother's wigs in my book bag along with a change of clothes. I changed and did my makeup to make me look older.

I entered the counselor's office. "Hello my name is, Crystal Stevens and I'm here for my first day as this school new therapist," I said. The receptionist replied, "I don't recall of anyone getting hired as the school therapist."

"Really, that's weird... I was given an interview the other day and was told to come back here today," I replied.

"And who was your interview with?" she asked. "Oh. Um, I'm sorry I've seemed to forget their name but I'm sure I should be in the system," I said. The receptionist starts tying on her computer. "Oh, here you are... Crystal Stevens. I apologize for the inconvenience you can just have a seat and I will prepare your desk," She replied.

I managed to hack the system and add my name to their roster. Not only that, but I was also able to create a fake diploma. Those are the perks I've picked up from information technology class. "You're desk is ready Ma'am, I apologize for the confusion once again they just never told me anything about a new school therapist," She said. "No worries, I am just happy to be here," I said as she walked me to my new office.

I took my seat at my new office and got straight to work. I placed each folder on my desk then began looking up my friends and their classes. One by one I called each person's teacher to see when would be a good time for each of them to meet with me. The first person that met with me was Mike. "Hi Mike how's it going, you may have a seat," I said as he walked inside. Mike nervously takes a seat on the reclining chair. "Am I in trouble?" Mike asked. "No no, of course not...dear, I just wanted to give you the chance to talk to me about any problems you've been facing here at this school? I asked. "Problems, what kind of problems?" he questioned. "Problems with teachers, students, anything you can think of," I said. "Oh I don't know, I don't feel like hearing my teacher's mouth," He replied. "Oh no Michael, what is said in this room stays in this room. If I break that I would be violating my license," I said. The mood suddenly became serious in the room, Mike looks up at me.

"The teachers are always trying to bring me down. Saying I'm not going to do nothing in life or be anything. I told my counselor I wanted to be in pre law class and she laughed at me, told me I should think more realistic," He said. "Wow I am so sorry, does that make you feel like they are right?" I asked.

"I don't know... are they? I'm failing all my classes," Mike said.

"Hmmp, Mike... I don't think you know how smart you really are," I said.

"And how would you know how smart I am?" He questioned.

"I can tell you are a very underestimated young man who I bet loves to win an argument," I said. Mike and I began to laugh.

"Yea, not only that but I actually know my stuff. I've read everything there is to know about being a lawyer but then I suddenly just stopped trying," Mike said.

"Mike, I'm going to tell you like I've told many of my friends. If you truly want something you have to tap in to that dream and use the strength inside of you to accomplish anything you want in life. Don't ever let anyone tell you, you can't something. I know for a fact that you can be a successful lawyer. I see it in you," I said. "Really?" Mike questioned.

After Mike left my office the next person to come in was, Iris. I haven't seen Iris since the 2nd floor at *Atlas Institution*. I eyes lit up as she walked through the doors. I was so happy to see her. "Hello Iris, please take a seat," I said. "My name is Mrs. Cyrstal and I just want to start off by saying what is said in my office remains in my office," I said. "Okay, I'm just trying to figure out why I was sent here in the first place?" Iris asked. "Well, I am just trying to speak to each student to discuss any problems you may have in this school?" I asked. "But what if I don't have any problems?" she explained. "Then that's great," I replied. "How are you liking it here at this High School?" I asked.

"It's okay." She replied.

"And what do you plan on doing after school?"

"Becoming a chemical scientist,"

"That's great, has this school helped you accomplish that goal?"

"Well, at the end of the day I believe it's up to me to accomplish that goal isn't it?"

"Yes, but don't you believe you need to have the right tools to study and become a chemical scientist?"

"Yea..I guess, can I leave now?"

"Yes, you may leave..thank you."

Iris was even more stubborn than before. She stormed out of my office.

I avoided my parents when I got home. I didn't want them to ask me any questions about school. I stayed in my room and studied information on each person. I went over their behaviors and reactions over certain things. My mom opened my door, "Have you seen my short wig?" she asked.

"No, maybe Yvette?" I asked.

"She's at Jocelyn's house; I'll ask her when she gets home. What are you working on anyway?" My mother asked. "I quickly put the folder away and moved my math book in front of me as smooth as possible. "Math class, you know…studying geometric shapes probability and statics… all that fun stuff," I said. "Okay, well you keep studying and there's food in the fridge when you get hungry," My mother said.

Yvette came barging in my room right before I was about to head to sleep. "Hey girl hey," She yelled. "It's late Yvette I'm trying to go to sleep," I replied. "Well wake up because we're going to a party tonight," She said. "No, I'm okay I have to catch up on my studying," I said. "Really, come on Angel have a little fun for once and stop thinking about school. It's not good for your health you know," Yvette said. I started laughing at her, "You know nothing about what's good for my health."

"I know one thing," She said as she takes a seat on my bed. "Mom and Dad went on a date night and we're free to stay out as long as we want. I know because she asked for about her short wig. Yea, that's her going out wig," Yvette said.

Yvette starts shaking me on the bed. "Get up, let's go," She begged. "Alright, alright.. I'm coming," I replied. I looked in my closet for something to wear. I honestly didn't even know how to dress for party like this. Yvette comes in my room wearing a skimping dress and tank top. "Okay, dress like a slut...noted," I said. "I heard that," Yvette replied. I laughed then changed my clothes. I wore a red dress with some red boots to match. "Yea sis!" Yvette said. "Now let's go!"

We arrived at the house party. Almost everyone from school was there. We parked the around the corner and walked to the house. People were already offering me liquor before I even made it to the door. "Yvette!" Jocelyn screamed. "Jocelyn parties?" I asked. "Yea girl, you must not know Jocelyn," Yvette replied. "Shots for you both," Jocelyn said while handing us each shot glasses. Yvette gulps down the shot. "You're driving!" I yelled. "It was only one shot," she explained. "Take yours," she said. I gulped my shot down. Yvette and Jocelyn laughs at me. "What have you never taking a shot before?" Jocelyn asked.

"Angel, is that you? I wouldn't have invited you if I knew you partied," Valerie said as she's running towards me. "Yea, my sister dragged me out the house," I replied. Valerie gives Yvette a high five, "Good Job Yvette," she said. "Come on let's go flirt with some boys," Valerie said. "Oh.. no no no," I replied nervously. Valerie takes me outside. All the guys were outside smoking blunts. We watched as three pickup trucks parked on the side of the street. Thomas and his friends get out the car. "What ever happened to guys, weren't ya'll like best friends?" Valerie asked. "I don't know Valerie you tell me, when did Thomas change?" I asked. "I have no idea...let's get drunk!" She screamed. Everyone outside cheered. A couple guys come over with a big keg. "I hear someone wants to get drunk?" the guy said. "Yes, this girl right here!" Valerie cheers. The guys lift her upside down while she chugged down the keg. They put Valerie down and she is pumped more than ever. "You're next, let's go," Valerie cheered. "Oh I don't think so..."

I started to say. Before I knew I was already upside down. "Chug, chug, chug, chug!" Everyone chanted! I chugged down the keg. The guys put me back on my feet and I could barely walk. I fell to the ground. "Oh my gosh are you okay?" Valerie asked. I burst into laughter. "I'm good!" I answered.

I danced with Valerie inside the house. I was starting to feel tipsy. I peeked over to the kitchen and noticed my sister taking another shot. I ran over to her. "Yvette, no more drinking...what the hell!" I yelled. Jocelyn starts laughing. "That's it, forget it...I'll just drive," I said.

"No, sis, I'm just joking. That was only my second shot, and my last. I really want you to have a good time," She said.

"Well I can't if I see you drinking," I said. Jocelyn continues to laugh.

"Why are you laughing Jocelyn she shouldn't be drinking if she's driving," I said. "Chill, she's fine...she knows her limit," She replied.

"Her limit?!" I yelled.

"Calm down I was just joking Angel," Jocelyn replied.

Yvette and Jocelyn left the kitchen to go dancing. I stood there for a minute to get some water. Thomas walks in and grabs a drink. My mouth had no filter at this point. "Hey Thomas, how's it going?" I asked.

"Great, enjoying the party," he replied.

"So when did you become a racist jerk?" I asked.

"What are you talking about I'm not racist," he replied.

Valerie runs over to me and covers my mouth. "Sorry, she's drunk," Valerie explained.

Valerie pulls me over to the dance floor.

"What are you doing, I'm not even drunk and I wanted to hear what he had to say," I argued.

"Not the right place for that, wait until you guys are alone to talk. You're killing the vibe here Angel," Valerie said.

I took Valerie's advice and just started enjoying the party. "Cops, Cops!" I heard someone yell. "Oh shit, let's go!" Valerie grabs my arm and we take off running. I hear police sirens get louder. I wasn't expecting this and almost shit myself. Everyone jumped in their car and drove off. I ran to the car. "Where is Yvette?!" I yelled. "What, I thought she would be here," Valerie said. We ran back in the party to find her and Jocelyn upstairs drunk with a couple of guys. "Did you guys not hear that Cops were outside!" I yelled. The guys got up and started running out the house. One guy was so drunk he ran into the door and didn't get back up. I pulled Yvette's arm while Valerie pulled Jocelyn's.

We ran to the backyard and jumped the fence because the cops were all over the front of the house. We hid behind a big bush. An officer with his flash light searches around the house. "Hey, Mat come look at this," Another officer said. The officer with his flash light left. We then ran behind a tree. We watched as the officer's were flashing the light a couple guys passed out on the floor. Yvette stars throwing up beside me. I put her on my back and ran to the car. "What the hell are you thinking?" I yelled. "I just took a couple shots," Yvette slurred. I was heated with anger. "And you, letting my sister get drunk when she's driving and then you two are up stairs with a bunch of guys!" What kind of best friend are you?" I yelled. "At lease I know how to act my age instead of an old grandma," Jocelyn replied. I balled my fist and started coming towards Jocelyn. "Angel, chill… they're drunk," Valerie said. I released my fist and helped the girls in the car. Jocelyn winked at me as she got inside. I ignored her and sat outside with Valerie. I waited for the Uber car to pick us up because I didn't trust myself to drive.

I woke up early the next morning to go pick up the car. By the time I got back Yvette was in the bathroom throwing up. "Sister… Sister… can you… help me," Yvette said as she's throwing up. I walked in the bathroom and tied her hair up. "You're lucky I love you," I said. "Hey, I just wanted to let you know it wasn't Jocelyn's fault I got drunk, it was mine. I took the shots, she didn't give them to me," She explained. "I don't care how it happened Yvette, I don't trust her," I replied. Yvette rinsed her face and we left the bathroom. "What's your problem with her?" Yvette asked. "I don't have a problem with her I just want you to be cautious of who you hang around. You need to surround yourself with people who only want the best for you," I said. I went to my room and shut the door. "Just give her a chance, please. She's my best friend and you know her mom is struggling Angel. She could use the support," Yvette yelled.

It was Sunday morning and the family and I got ready to go to church. We all got into my dad's car. "Why aren't we leaving?" I asked as we all sat in the car. "We're waiting for Jocelyn," Yvette replied. I rolled my eyes. "There she is," Yvette said. Yvette opens the door for Jocelyn. "Good morning everyone," Jocelyn said. "Good morning Jocelyn, are you ready for church?" my dad asked. "Yes I am," she replied.

We rejoiced and sang in church. We broke bread and drank cranberry juice for Jesus Christ. The pastor stands at his podium. "Let us rise and hold hands," The pastor said. "Let us all come together to celebrate the life of Jesus Christ, our savior. Let us all lift each other up in the name of the lord. Let us let go of any grudges against our brothers and sisters. Let us open our hearts for forgiveness," The pastor preached. Jocelyn squeezed my hand when he said forgiveness.

When the service was over Jocelyn pulls me over to the side. "I'm sorry about last night Angel, I don't know what I was thinking," She said. "It's okay Jocelyn, I forgive you," I replied. "It really hurts when you're upset with me, I mean… you are and have always been like a big sister to me," She explained. "Aww that's sweet, come here," I said as I gave her a hug. "Yes, I've been waiting for this," Yvette said. Yvette joins in and we all give each other one big hug.

It was Monday morning and I was back in my office as the school therapist. My first student on the list was Thomas. "Thomas Bebe, Good Morning… you may have a seat," I said. "Do you have any idea why you are here today?" I asked. "Nope, but there is something I wanted to talk about," he said. "Oh yes… the floor is all yours," I replied. "So my childhood friend called my racist the other day and I can't seem to get it through my head. I'm not racist. I think she just said that because we no longer hang out like we use to when we were younger," He explained. "And why is that?" I asked. "I don't know…she has her friends and I have mine," He said. "Hmm, question Thomas.. How does your friends feel about your child hood friend?" I asked. "They.. they… are cool with her," he said. "Really?" I asked. "No, they are the ones who are racist," I explained. "Ahh, so is that the reason why you no longer associate yourself with your child hood friend?" I asked. "Kinda…because my parents always had something to say and now my friends and I just don't feel like hearing their mouths," He said. "So that means you don't say anything at all? How does your friend feel about this?" I asked. "Well to start off, her and I are no longer friends," Thomas said. "Ohh so it's a her huh, and how did she take that?" I asked. "I could tell she was hurt and that is never my intention," Thomas said.

"I just don't know what to do at this point and I wish I could tell her that I'm sorry," Thomas said. I could no longer hold it in. I took my wig off to reveal myself.

"Thomas, it's me."

"Angel? What are you doing impersonating a therapist. Did you know I was going to come here and talk about you? You've lost it," Thomas gets out his chair.

"Thomas, sit down."

I waited for Thomas so slowly take his seat.

"No, I did not do this because I knew you were going to come here to talk about me. How could I possibility even know that? Thomas, what if I told you that you and I weren't just child hood friends? What I told you that we've have been best friends for years and you just don't remember?"

"What, why wouldn't I remember?"

"Because we were on a different universe and the vortex exploded and sent us back in time."

"Okay, you have really lost it," Thomas begins to get out his seat.

"Thomas you have never believed me all throughout our friendship. You always thought I made up stories or was over reacting. You have got to believe me this time. Please, I just ask you to try to remember. If you really care about me and our friendship like you say you do, that's all that I'm asking from you. Just try to remember," I said.

Thomas leaves my office. I put my wig back on and took a deep breath.

I decided to take a break from my office and get some lunch. I sat with the rest of the teachers in the break room. I noticed the principal having a conversation with the receptionist from the counselor's office. She then points at me and my stomach drops. "Mrs. Stevens is it?" The principal asked.

"Yes, that is me."

"I am sorry Mrs. Stevens but there must have been an error in our system, we are going to have to ask you to leave."

Two police officers start walking towards me.

"If you do refuse to leave we are going to have to get law enforcement involved," The principal said.

"No, no...there's no need for that. I'll be leaving right away," I said.

I ran to the restroom before anyone could see me. I quickly changed my clothes and took off my wig. I then remembered I left my papers in my office. I ran upstairs before they could confiscate my belongings. "How may I help you?" the receptionist asked. "Oh I seemed to have left something in Mrs. Steven's office I just want to go get it really quick," I said as I continued walking. I wasn't going to take no for an answer. I found my papers right where I left them. I walked out the office and headed to the front. That's when I noticed Thomas. I stood in the back but was close enough to hear their conversation. "I'm here to see Mrs. Stevens," Thomas said. "Mrs. Stevens is no longer working here, I'm sorry," The receptionist said. "What do you mean, she was just hear a couple of hours ago," Thomas said. "Yes, but we had some complications with our computer system and unfortunately we had to let her go," She replied.

I waited for Thomas to leave the office. "Thank you," I said to the receptionist while rushing out the office. I put my back against the wall and took a couple deep breaths. The bell rang and it was time for Gym class. In Gym class today we were having a fun game of doge ball. It was one side of the room verses the other. It was a tied game with two people on each side, me being one of them. I grabbed the dodge ball and concentrated. I aimed the ball for my opponent. I threw the ball and the ball froze in mid air then started moving in slow motion. My force was too strong. I was viewing the future of my classmates once again. There were so many visions I couldn't handle viewing them all at once. I ran into the locker room. I hid myself in my locker and tried to block out the loud sounds of the students. I tried my best to relax my body. I changed my clothes and left the locker room. The noise became even stronger as I walked through the halls. I ran out the building and went home early.

My mom cooked my favorite meal for dinner because I was passing all of my classes with straight A's. "Did you hear about the lady who impersonated a school therapist?" Yvette asked. "No, what happened?" I asked as if I didn't know. "There are guessing that she hacked the computer system because she just magically appeared on their roster one day and she told the lady at the front desk that she had an interview for the position and was hired. She even had one on one session's with students,"

Yvette explained. "Well, what did the students have to say about her?" My dad asked.

"I think we are about to find out right now," My mom said as she turns on the news.

"Woman hacks computer system and impersonates school therapist" Was the headline going across the screen. A reporter was interviewing students outside the school. "What was Mrs. Stevens saying to you?" the reporter asked. "Well she told me to tap in to my full potential and focus on school because it will help me in the future," A student said. Mike runs in front of the camera. "She told me not to listen to what anyone has to say about me and if I want to be a lawyer, I'm going to be a lawyer got damn it.. ouu, sorry mom," Mike said. The reporter laughs, "Thomas, can you tell us about your one on one session with Mrs. Stevens?" The reporter asked. "Oh look, it's Thomas," My mother said. "She made me realize a lot of things about myself that I didn't even realize. She is an Angel sent to school," Thomas said. "Well, there you have it folks, an Angel sent to their High School," The reporter said. My mother turned off the TV.

The next morning I woke up and wouldn't dare step foot in that school again. I couldn't handle the visions all at once. "Mom I'm really sick again, I can't make it to school," I whimpered. "Sick my ass, you've already missed too many days. You're going to school," She said. I huffed and puffed all my belongings together for school. I kicked my shelf out of frustration, knocking over my nail polish. I bent down to pick up my nail polish then noticed my book bag from *Atlas Institution* under my bed. My book bag must have made it back with me when I was destroying the vortex. I looked inside to find a bunch of notes and fake money from Mr. Jamisons class. I looked at the money once more. The money may have been fake at *Atlas Institution* but it sure did look real on Earth. If I was, I was 50,000 richer. I gathered everything and headed to school, or at lease told my mother that's where I was heading.

My mother was still getting ready to work. "Enjoy High School while you can Angel, you'll miss it once you leave," My mother said as I walked towards the door.

"Do you miss your High School?" I asked her.

"Oh, I wouldn't say I even went to high school…it was more of training school. You're father and I went right after we had you, but sadly I am slowly losing my memory of it. I'm getting older. It is really bitter sweet though because I wasn't able to enjoy high school as a teenager but I was able to provide for you and your sister and that's all that mattered," My mother said. "Mom, did you ever see your friends at school and could almost tell their future wasn't going to be so bright by the path they were taking?" I asked.

"All the time," She replied.

"Did you try to help them?" I asked.

"A few more times than I should have actually. Angel, you are going to realize one day that you can't save everyone and you can't control the fate of anyone's future... only they can," My mother said.

"Right," I said and slowly grabbed the door knob.

I began opening the door. "One more question?" I asked.

"Go ahead," she said.

"Do you think you could have accomplished everything you have today without that training school? I asked.

"Of course, but it was my choice to study there because your father and I knew exactly what we wanted for the future," She said.

"Thanks mom," I said and walked out the house.

I couldn't go to school, I desperately needed to gather my thoughts before I lose my sanity and hearing from attending that school. I thought I'd give this money a try and headed to the mall. My first purchase was something small; I brought a t-shirt. The cashier took my money and lifted it in the air to see if it was real or not. She puts the money in the drawer and bags my t-shirt. The transaction went through.

I walked into my favorite clothing store. I brought everything I wanted to buy but tried not to go overboard. I was the happiest girl on the planet. I went to get ice cream after shopping. I sat down in the mall cafeteria. I looked at the empty seats besides me. I may have had a lot of money but I started to feel empty inside from being alone and not having anyone to talk to about my problems.

I went back home and spread my money on the table. I thought about the moment Mr. Jamison gave us this money. I never imagined this money helping me on earth. I thought about my options with this money. I thought about all the investments other students used with their money. I also thought about just taking this money and moving to another state to start over. I had to make a decision before my family returned home.

I couldn't explain to them how I got this money and I couldn't tell my mom why I couldn't go to high school anymore. I decided to use my money to invest in a training program for students. This way it would help students with their future careers but unlike *Atlas Institution*, the students would have the choice to stay in the program or leave. This way was sure to fix the damage I have done.

For the next couple months my mother thought I was going to school every morning when instead I was meeting with the school officials to start my new training program. They all looked at me crazy because I was so young but I felt like I've lived a long life. Yvette didn't catch on until the second month but I took her on a shopping spree so she would keep her mouth shut. A few more months pass by and my new training program is up and ready. I have already covered a news story and it was going to air tonight. I ran home and couldn't wait to tell my parents my biggest accomplishment before they heard it on the news for themselves.

I walked in the house and my mom and dad was sitting at the table. "Angel, have a seat," My dad said. "We talked to your teachers Angel, turns out you haven't been attending the whole semester and they have withdrawn you from school. We did not work our butts off for you to throw everything away!" My mother raised her voice. "Okay, before you guys get upset I have a reason behind all of this. I have created a training program and it is finally open for the public," I explained.

Their faces went blank and they weren't buying the news. "Angel, you and these lies have got to stop," My dad said. "I'm not lying I really built a school so students could train while they study," I said. "Yea right on what universe do you think we're on?" My dad said. "I don't know, maybe I think you're back *Atlas Institution*," I couldn't hold it in. "*Atlas Institution*, that was it... how did you know that?" My mother asked. "Because I went to *Atlas Institution* and I destroyed the vortex and now I am only trying to make things right," I said.

"Breaking new, young teen opens up a training program for students to better their future," We heard from the TV. My parents jaw dropped as they watched me on screen. My sister and Jocelyn ran through the doors. "Is it true? That's what you were doing the whole time?" Yvette asked. We watched my interview on TV. "Angel, how did you even do this?" My mother asked. "Mr. Jamison's math class had an investment project and he let me keep the money at the end. So I used the money to invest in this," I said. "Mr. Jamison... he is still there?" My father asked. "Not anymore...not after I destroyed the school and returned everyone back to earth," I said.

A couple months later and I was presented with the key to the city. "To the youngest entrepreneur this city has seen. We present you, Angel Myers, the key to the city," the governor said. I took my plague and watched my friends in the crowd cheer for me. "I just want to say, thank you for presenting me with the key to the city. This is my biggest accomplishment I have ever achieved. And to anyone who plans on enrolling in my training program, just know that we are there to help you in your journey to your bright future. We encourage all students to tap in to their highest potential while attending this program. To think above and beyond the normal standards of life. You are truly able to do whatever you seek, all you have to do is put in the work. Thank you everyone."

With my alone time I learned to challenge my powers. I was able to see people's future but it was easier for me to turn it on and off. My school was up and running and I was finally feeling like I could be at peace. That night my mother made another one of my favorite meals. I could never get tired of my mother's cooking. "That's the door hunny can you get that," My dad said. My mother was already standing up; she walked over to the front door. "Come on in," She said. "Hey, Jocelyn...take a seat," My dad said. The door bell rang once more. "Who could that be?" my mother asked as she goes over to open the door. "Oh wow, look who is it...I haven't seen you since you were a little boy," my mother said. Thomas walks through the doors. "I thought I could join you guys for dinner, you know...just like old times," Thomas said. We all looked over at my dad's reaction. "It's okay with me if it's okay with Angel," My dad said. I smiled, "Yea, its okay with me," and we all ate dinner together.

"Thank you for the dinner," Jocelyn said as my sister walks her out. Thomas and I talked like it was old times and nothing ever changed. "See you tomorrow?" Thomas asked as he stood at the door. "Ehh, I don't know," I said. I started laughing after looking at Thomas's disappointing face. "I'm just joking, I'll see you tomorrow," I said. "Alright, see ya," Thomas said. I shut the door and headed to my bed. No more trying to alter the fate of anyone's future for me. It was now time for me to focus on my own future.

Jocelyn headed home. She was relieved to finally get in her pajamas after a long day. She takes off her contacts. Her eyes appeared to be the same color as Angel's. Jocelyn was keeping a very big secret. She was given the power from the vortex just like Angel. She walks in her room and there are diagrams and space ship drawings all over her room. Jocelyn was coming up with a plan of her own. Jocelyn turns off the lights and heads to bed.

You're future starts now.

Printed in the United States
By Bookmasters